CW00421438

Blackwater Lake

MAGGIE JAMES

Published 2019 by Orelia Publishing.

Chapter 1 - *Missing*

'When did you realise your parents were missing, Mr Stanyer?'

Too late, Matthew thought; he should have checked on them sooner. The words *bad son* bounded through his brain, flooding him with guilt.

'Mr Stanyer?' Detective Sergeant Hutton's fingertips rapped on the table, recapturing his attention. *Focus*, he told himself.

'When I went to their house this morning.'

'And how long has it been since you last talked to them?'

'Thursday. Dad was supposed to phone me yesterday. But he didn't.'

'You're not close?' Did he hear censure in Hutton's voice?

Matthew shrugged. 'I've not seen much of them since I left home at eighteen. Apart from after I returned to Bristol twelve months ago.'

'But you only live half a mile from them?' Oh, yeah, that was censure all right. Screw Hutton. What the hell did the guy know? How would the judgemental bastard understand what kept him from visiting his parents? The... *monstrosity*... that meant he hated entering the house in which he grew up. Apart from last year, when necessity had forced his hand, he spent as little time there as possible. College in London had lured him away once he reached adulthood, then came a succession of

1

mundane jobs followed by travel. On his second trip around Europe he discovered the joys of sub-aqua, leading to a decade in Crete as a diving instructor. His mother's illness was what clawed him back a year ago.

Impossible to explain his aversion to his childhood home to Hutton. Besides, the police would search the place. When they did, they'd see for themselves.

He forced his voice to stay calm. 'You're right; we're not close. I've done my best, though. To help them.'

'So what prompted you to go there today?' Hutton queried. Onion-tainted breath wafted towards Matthew.

He shifted in his seat, so far out of his comfort zone he was almost in orbit. God, the room was hot. Sweat dampened his armpits, moistened his collar. He wondered what Hutton saw as the police officer stared at him. Someone stressed, no doubt, pale with worry and tension. As for the rest: thirty-five years old, six feet one, lean as a lurcher. Hair a shade away from black, flopping over brown eyes.

'Johnny Depp meets Orlando Bloom,' Lauren had once told him. 'Quite the cutie, aren't you, babe?'

He leaned back, away from the onion breath. 'Like I said, Dad promised to phone me. Mum's been getting worse. The illness is progressing rapidly. It's been...' He swallowed hard. 'Difficult for him. He has to leave her alone when he goes to work. He said he'd call. But he didn't.'

'Did you try his mobile?'

'Dad doesn't have one. They're both dinosaurs with technology.'

'So you went to the house?'

'Yes. That's when I found the note.' Matthew gestured across the table. A sheet of A5, scrawled with his father's handwriting, lay in front of Hutton. When he first read its words, Matthew's stomach had turned to ice.

'Son. Your mother and I can't go on this way. I'm doing what I believe is best. God knows we've not always done the right thing. I'm sorry. About everything.'

'You can understand why I'm worried,' he said.

'You mentioned your father had concerns over his employment?'

'Yes. It's a physical job, you see. Blackwater Park isn't large, but being its groundsman involves a lot of manual labour. And he's sixty. Suffers back pain, arthritic knees. He might have to retire soon.'

'Would that be a problem financially? Did he have money worries?'

'Yes. Dad's never earned much. I doubt he's ever paid into a pension.'

'Any living relatives beside yourself?'

Matthew shook his head. 'No. What's the next step? To finding them?'

'We need photos of your parents. We'll also search their house, see if we can find any clues as to where they've gone.'

Shit. He'd realised the police would check his parents' home, but that didn't prevent his gut clamping with embarrassment. The house in which he grew up, the source of his shame. The reason he'd never taken Lauren, his girlfriend of six months, to meet Joe and Evie Stanyer. Within the next few hours, his parents' secret would be exposed, like a tumour highlighted by a scan. Dear God. They were dead. Had to be. They'd never suffer strangers in the house otherwise.

'Let me run over the basics again,' Hutton said. 'Make sure we've got the facts straight.'

Matthew listened as Hutton recapped what he'd already been told. Both parents apparently missing. Father Joseph Stanyer, known as Joe, aged sixty. Height five eleven, thin to the point of gauntness. Slight limp due to his arthritis. Pasty complexion, brown eyes. Bald on top, remaining hair grey. Sole groundsman at the Blackwater estate. Mother Evie Stanyer, aged fifty-five but looked older. Five eight, carrying twenty excess kilos on her belly and thighs. Hair faded to silver, eyes dimmed to pale blue. A housewife before her illness. Now she didn't do much of anything.

'I'll send someone to your parents' house right away,' Hutton said. 'Can you meet us there?'

He must have clocked the reluctance shadowing Matthew's face. 'Problem? Something I should know about?'

'Yes. No. It's complicated.' Matthew huffed out a breath. 'You'll understand soon enough.' Hutton's eyebrows rose, but he didn't comment further.

'Your parents' disappearance will be high priority,' he said. 'What with your mother being what we call vulnerable.'

Matthew nodded. Evie Stanyer was vulnerable, all right. What else could you call a fifty-five-year-old woman with premature dementia?

*****

His thoughts reeled back to his visit earlier that day, the one that prompted him to report his parents missing. Sunday morning at his flat, kicked off by fierce sex with Lauren, their bodies slick with sweat afterwards. Once his post-coital haze dispersed, worry nagged at Matthew's mind. His father hadn't phoned, despite his promise. When they spoke on Thursday, Joe Stanyer told his son he'd call Saturday evening. There were matters, important ones, for them to discuss. Neither of them had voiced the words 'care home', but things couldn't go on as they were, not with Mum getting worse by the week.

The last time he'd seen his parents, his father had left Matthew alone with Evie, saying he needed to prune the roses in the back garden. His son knew better, however. Joe was desperate for a break from his wife, the woman he bathed, dressed, took to the toilet, on top of a forty-hour working week.

His mother's fingers plucked at the chintz fabric of the armchair.

'Such beautiful hair, she had,' she said.

'Who?'

Without warning, Evie's eyes narrowed. Spite snaked into them, startling Matthew into inching backwards, shocked by the malice in her expression. She looked ready to kill. With savage speed, his mother grasped his arm, pinching it hard.

'She deserved everything she got,' she hissed. 'The little whore should have kept her legs shut.'

'Be quiet, Evie, for God's sake!' Joe's voice boomed from the doorway, his anger startling Matthew. He'd not heard him come in from the garden.

'Don't, Dad. She can't help it.'

Joe drew in a breath. 'Sorry, son. Just gets to me at times, it does.'

'I understand.' He did, too. It was hard these days to spend an hour with his mother. Impossible to imagine what his dad must endure daily. Now wasn't the time to discuss a care facility, though. Soon, Matthew promised himself. When he next visited, he'd get the ball rolling.

How could he know he'd never see his parents alive again?

Lauren tapped a finger against Matthew's chest. 'Penny for your thoughts, handsome.' The silk of her hair lay cool against his stubble, the scent of her shampoo teasing his nostrils. Lauren Cooper, so uncomplicated, so different to the women he'd dated in Greece. Ah, Crete. God, he missed Heraklion. The dive school where he'd taught for ten years. The smell of fish, fresh from the day's catch. Lamb kebabs, thick with onions and peppers, washed down with Pezan wine. A shade over twelve months had passed since he'd left; what he wouldn't give to return. If and when he did, chances were he'd ask Lauren to go with him.

They'd met at the food market held in Bristol's Corn Street, not far from the diving shop where he worked. Her range of homemade pies were what drew his eye at first, until he checked her out. Thirty years old, a smidgen shy of six feet, her hair a rich caramel, her irises pools of soft aquamarine. Brown eyes met blue, and they chatted. He learned Lauren was an art teacher, with the pies being a sideline. From somewhere he found the guts to ask her out and that night they ended up in bed, the sex hard and urgent. Now he was hooked, and not just because of her skill with pastry.

Matthew realised she was waiting for an answer. 'Not heard from Dad for a few days, that's all.'

'He's probably just forgotten. Why don't you phone him later?'

'Yeah, I'll do that. I need to make sure they're both OK.'

After Lauren left, he called his parents' house, listening to the ringtone a dozen times before giving up. Anxiety clawed at Matthew's stomach. If his father hadn't called him as arranged, and wasn't answering the phone, then something was wrong. Very wrong. Had Dad suffered a heart attack? Or Mum a stroke? Either one of them, or both, might need urgent medical attention. Time to get his butt over there. He grabbed his jacket and keys.

Once in Blackwater Drive, he parked outside their house, the source of so much embarrassment during his childhood. He stared at the peeling paint on the windowsills, summoning the courage to go inside. The thought of his father, possibly unconscious, eventually shamed him into getting out of the car. Matthew strode towards the front door, inserting his key in the lock. He pushed against the wood, moving it ajar an inch.

'Dad? Are you there?' Silence. 'Hello?' Still no response. He pressed harder, shoving the door back a foot or so. Difficult to open it any further; its path was blocked. Through the gap, Matthew stared into his parents' house, one hand clamped over his nostrils to mask the odour that met him.

On either side of the hallway were boxes, crates, bags, together with all manner of ephemera. The cardboard boxes were old, filthy, the lower ones sagging under the weight of those above. Stacks of newspapers, their edges yellow and brittle, were interspersed amongst the chaos. To his left were several tea chests labelled 'books' in his mother's handwriting. His gaze travelled upwards over the stacks, noting the lack of gap between the ceiling and whatever lay underneath. Magazines, books and folders, all draped in cobwebs, competed for the available space, creating a solid wall of junk. Only a narrow path through the centre allowed access to the kitchen, from where a shaft of sunlight reached his eyes. Dust motes drifted through its beam.

This was Matthew's shame, the reason he'd left home the minute he could. Evie Stanyer was a hoarder. How the hell could he explain the way his parents lived to anyone?

He had never understood the reason for her compulsion. Oh, he'd read all the theories about why people hoarded. How the trait could be triggered by a traumatic event. Chalk one up to Evie on that score; his maternal grandparents had died in a car crash when she was eighteen. Tragedy wasn't the only cause; it seemed hoarding was often linked with certain psychological conditions. Again, Evie qualified; throughout her adult life she'd suffered anxiety attacks. Were her magpie habits linked to them, or to her parents' premature deaths?

The rest of the house was equally crammed with junk. The front room was the worst; he remembered when it still retained space to move, a time long since past. He didn't need to push against the door and peer round it to know it was now full.

The back room wasn't much better. Once Matthew had inched along the hallway and opened the door, he flicked on the light. No chance of seeing daylight through the windows, thanks to the hoard blocking them. Dust covered most of the room's contents. Enough space remained to squeeze in a couple of armchairs, either side of which more crates and boxes were stacked towards the ceiling. Along with the books, clothes and newspapers, food was Evie Stanyer's hoarding vice. Cans of tuna, bottled water, tins of beans; Matthew sometimes wondered whether his mother was preparing for an apocalypse. Somehow he'd expected to find his parents here, in the battered chintz armchairs, their ears attuned to the radio Matthew bought them last

Christmas. No TV, although the ancient portable, long since defunct, still stood on a side table. They'd not replaced it, being nervous of digital technology; the analogue radio had taken its place.

Matthew breathed in the stale odour. Less offensive than that of the hallway. Pulling the door closed, he walked into the kitchen.

Across the floor, the source of the stench met his eyes. An open bin bag, squatting by the back door, flies buzzing around rotting potato peelings. Beside it was a cluster of mouse droppings, topped with dust and hair. Dead wasps lined the windowsill. Dirty plates, pots and pans covered the available work surfaces and filled the sink.

Christ. Things had got worse, much worse, since his last visit a week ago. He retreated to the hallway, moving up the stairs as fast as the piles of junk allowed.

'Dad? Mum?' Stupid to expect a reply. The place possessed that eerie quality of emptiness despite being anything but. A quick glance sufficed for the bathroom and back bedroom. Then he opened the door to his parents' room.

Empty. Of them, anyway. Like the rest of the house, it was crammed full. Piles of bedding, an ancient dressmaker's dummy, his baby crib, stacks of other stuff. A damp, musty smell hung in the air. No sign of Evie and Joe Stanyer, though.

Matthew noticed something odd about the bed. Only one pillow. On it lay a piece of paper. His father's farewell message, the one he'd later give to Hutton.

Within the hour, he was at Bristol's Bridewell police station, reporting his parents as missing.

Chapter 2 - *Found*

'Christ.' Bewilderment in Detective Rawlins's tone. 'You hear of this sort of thing. But you don't realise, not until you see it…' The young police officer shook his head.

Matthew stood in the hallway to his parents' house. Hutton was in the kitchen. Behind him the fetid bin bag still buzzed with flies. Rawlins perched on the stairs, his body angled awkwardly over the boxes piled against the banister.

'Yeah, well, when you've logged as many years in the force as me, Rawlins, you'll have seen a thing or two, all right,' Hutton shot back. 'Mind you, I've never set eyes on hoarding this bad. Must be decades' worth of stuff here.' He opened a cupboard, took out a can of tomatoes. 'Christ. Three years out of date.' He walked towards Matthew. 'They've lived this way a long time, I take it?'

'Never known them to be any different.' He found it hard to meet Hutton's gaze. Odds were the man now realised the futility of searching the house. If clues to the Stanyers' whereabouts existed within the hoard, its piles of junk wouldn't yield them easily.

His next words confirmed Matthew's suspicions.

'Can't think we'll find much here,' Hutton said. 'We've done a preliminary check, as far as we can, and nothing's come to light. You got any idea where your father might have taken your mother?'

'Not really. Dad only left the house for two reasons. One was to buy groceries. His job was the other.'

Hutton edged closer. Another waft of onion breath hit Matthew's nostrils. 'Mrs Stanyer didn't go out?'

'No. She's always been a home bird. Besides, she's been getting more difficult to handle. Not uncommon with dementia patients.'

'Bit young for that, isn't she?'

Matthew shrugged. 'It strikes some people early. The symptoms began in her early fifties. Recently they've escalated.'

'We'll get a team searching at Blackwater Park. Might as well start there. We've already ruled out the hospitals. Meanwhile, do you have a recent photo of them?'

*****

He'd not known about his mother's dementia until her symptoms were well advanced. Ensconced in his life in Greece, a weekly phone call was his only interaction with his parents and it took a while before he understood why his mother sounded increasingly strange when he called her. Sometimes he'd be talking and when he finished, she didn't reply. 'Mum? Are you still there?' he'd ask, and she'd respond vaguely, and then his father would come on the line.

At first he'd put it down to tiredness, unwilling to consider whether her anxiety issues might be rearing their head again. Over time he'd accustomed himself to the change and hardly noticed her lapses, as he called them. When his birthday rolled around, and his card was signed by his father instead of both his parents, he thought it odd, but didn't comment. Later he wondered how he'd been so oblivious.

Then one evening his father rang him. An unprecedented event, causing Matthew's stomach to clench with apprehension. The norm was he'd phone home once a week, his mother answered, and afterwards he talked with his father.

'What's wrong, Dad? Is Mum OK?'

His father cleared his throat. 'You need to come home, son. Your mother's ill. I'll explain when you get here.'

*****

Back in Blackwater, Matthew stayed at a hotel whilst finding a flat to rent. No point in asking his father about his former bedroom; junk had claimed it long ago. When he set foot in his parents' home after over a decade away, shock chased the breath from his lungs. The hoard had grown exponentially, and then some. Boxes choked the hallway and stairs. For the first time, he needed to turn sideways to inch his way along the narrow passage, closing his nostrils against the stale odour from the piles of junk.

'Christ, Dad,' he managed. Joe Stanyer didn't respond.

The back room was where his mother spent her days and when Matthew saw her, shock froze the greeting on his lips. Whatever he'd been dreading, this exceeded his worst fears. Evie Stanyer had shrunk in every way. Her shoulders were hunched towards her ears, her back rounded, like she was a turtle retracting its head. The grooves between her nose and mouth had deepened to crevasses, as had her crow's feet. Smudges of ill health darkened the skin under her eyes. Her dishevelled hair had greyed to silver; her complexion resembled uncooked dough. His mother made no movement as he entered the room, her gaze fixed on her lap.

'Mum?' No response. He squeezed past a pile of boxes to kneel by her chair. Her vacant stare didn't waver. He reached out, touching the pale blue cardigan she wore, his fingers sensing the frailty of the forearm underneath. 'Mum, are you all right? It's me, Matty.'

Evie Stanyer's head turned towards him, slowly, as though she were afraid her neck might snap. 'Son? Is that you?' Her gaze was unfocused, glassy. 'What are you doing back so soon?'

He forced himself to stay calm as he stood up. Who the hell was this woman? Not his mother, that was for sure.

'I'll make us all some tea,' Joe Stanyer said.

Matthew watched from the doorway of the kitchen whilst his father busied himself with kettle and mugs. He appeared decades older, the bags under his eyes heavier, his jowls sagging. His bald patch now extended over most of his head, his remaining hair grey and unkempt. Like that of his wife, his skin exhibited an unhealthy quality. He'd lost weight, when he had none to spare, and Matthew's stomach clenched with worry. What on earth was going on?

He inched his way into the kitchen, noting the grease browning the stove. The pile of dishes in the sink, the unwashed pots and pans. The filthy tea towel used by Joe to give a cursory wipe to the mugs. A solitary fly buzzed against the window.

'What's wrong with Mum?'

His father poured boiling water onto the teabags, giving no sign he'd heard. Matthew took the mug offered to him, repelled by its stained rim.

'Talk to me. Has her anxiety got worse?'

Joe Stanyer sipped his tea. 'She's not been herself. Forgetting things, in a world of her own at times. At first, I didn't pay it much attention. Then one day she hit me.'

His father's words stunned Matthew. He'd have bet his life savings on his mother being incapable of violence, much less towards the husband she loved. 'Why? What happened?'

'She'd become fixated with Radio 2. Listened to it all the time. I fancied a change. Mentioned trying Radio Bristol. That's when she lashed out at me. Caught me with her fist, right in the ribs. It bloody well hurt, as you can imagine.'

Matthew chewed his bottom lip. His father's words made no sense.

'That's when I realised,' Joe continued. 'Didn't want to admit it, though.'

'Admit what?'

'Your mother's got dementia.'

Matthew drew in a shocked breath. 'That can't be right. She's only in her fifties.'

'Happens that way sometimes, son. It's unusual for someone her age to develop it, but it's not unheard of.'

When Matthew didn't reply, Joe Stanyer said, 'After she punched me, I forced her to go to her doctor. They did tests at the hospital. She didn't do well on them. Couldn't remember what month or year it was. A brain scan helped confirm the diagnosis. Early onset Alzheimer's, progressing rapidly.'

'Oh, my God.' Matthew thought about his mother hunched in her chair. Those glassy, blank eyes, the rounded shoulders. Sadness swept over him when he remembered the woman who used to swing him around by the arms when he was little, who'd play hide and seek with him for hours. Following on the heels of sadness came regret, thick and bitter. Why hadn't he visited more often? Spent more time with the mother he loved, despite her eccentricities?

'What's the prognosis?' he asked, fighting to keep his voice steady.

'They tell me she'll need a care facility. Sooner rather than later. She's becoming more aggressive.' His father rolled up his sleeve, revealing a purple bruise that bloomed on his forearm. 'She did that yesterday. All I said was how

I'd cook cod and chips for supper, but she took a swing at me. Screamed she wanted lamb chops, not fish, and who the fuck did I think I was, deciding what she ate?'

Fresh shock hit Matthew. His mother never swore. 'Is violence common with dementia sufferers?'

'Her doctor told me some people change personality altogether. Seems she might be one of them.' His father shut his eyes, pinching his nose, and Matthew realised Joe Stanyer's lids were leaking tears. The sight rattled him. Badly.

'Don't know how much longer I can cope, son. She needs constant care, impossible with me still working. The thought of her in one of those places, though...' He swallowed. 'Well, you hear such things. Not always good.'

Matthew tried to wrap his brain around the situation. His mother shouldn't be left alone whilst her husband went to work. The house lacked a downstairs toilet; the boxes on the stairs rendered them hazardous even for the able-bodied. Far worse for a disorientated and frail woman.

'Matty? Is that you?' Evie Stanyer's voice cut into his thoughts. He edged his way back to his mother, the woman who had comforted him after the childhood fall that sliced his chin. Who, for years afterwards, kissed the scar at bedtimes. Now slumped in her armchair, her grip on reality fading.

'You don't visit enough,' she said.

She was right, of course. Guilt cut through him; he'd allowed the hoard to keep him away, leaving his father to cope with a sick wife by himself. Something needed to change. Time to man up; now he was back in the UK he'd be a better son, give his parents the support they required.

Silence for a while. Matthew wanted to voice his new-found resolution, but hadn't a clue how to frame the words. And if he did, would she even understand?

His mother's fingers picked at her cardigan. Still unsure what to say, he reached out, taking her hand, pressing it lightly.

'I'm sorry,' he said, his voice hoarse.

It was as though he'd not spoken. 'Never been able to forgive myself.' Evie's voice was plaintive.

Matthew waited. When she didn't continue, he asked, his tone gentle, 'What for, Mum?'

His mother reached up a sleeve, wiped uselessly at her cheek, her eyes soaked with tears.

'I swore not to tell. So did your father. It wasn't right, though. What we did.'

'Don't upset yourself, Mum. Please.'

'Can't get the image out of my head.' Her gaze slid away.

She was rambling, of course; only to be expected with the dementia. Matthew touched her arm. 'I'll bring you some tea.'

*****

Afterwards, he visited every week. His father began phoning on alternate days, sounding increasingly defeated and exhausted. His wife's illness was progressing rapidly, her aggressive spells more frequent. If Matthew mentioned getting Evie into a care facility, Joe became evasive, though.

'Somewhere good won't come cheap. Where do I find the money?'

'Have you considered a council-run place?'

His father snorted. 'You know how strapped for money the NHS is. Those places are a last resort.'

'Home-based care?' Matthew regretted his stupidity as soon as the words left his mouth. No agency would ever send carers to the house, not with the hoard choking it.

Most times he visited, his mother appeared withdrawn, as though someone had dimmed her lights. Sometimes she recognised him, often not. The first time she called him by his father's name, he tried, without success, not to be affected. He might not be an ideal son, but hell, she was his mother. She should damn well recognise him.

'Doesn't work that way, babe.' He'd met Lauren by then. Thanks to her grandmother's Alzheimer's, his girlfriend was no stranger to the cruelties of the illness. Whilst on a logical level he knew she was right, on an emotional plane it didn't help. Every time he visited his mother, sadness and regret filled the room, a constant rebuke for his failure to be a good son.

*****

'I'm worried sick,' Matthew told Lauren Sunday night, after DS Hutton told him to go home, that he'd be in touch. 'They've always been such home birds, rarely venturing out of Blackwater. Something bad has happened, I'm sure.'

In response, his girlfriend wrapped her arms around him, hugging him close. He was grateful for the fact she didn't offer platitudes, trite assurances his parents would be found safe and well, with some logical reason for their disappearance. Because if an explanation existed, he couldn't think of one. Joe and Evie Stanyer never stayed away overnight, and if his father had taken his wife somewhere, why wouldn't he have told his son?

Small wonder he had a bad gut feeling about this.

*****

The day after he reported his parents as missing, Hutton called at his flat, briefing him on the police's progress so far. Which was none.

'What happens now?' asked Matthew. 'You've sent a team to Blackwater Park, right?'

'Dispatched a search party there earlier. I'll call you if there's any news.'

'Thanks.' It hadn't been necessary, though. Hutton's phone rang. He moved into the hallway, out of Matthew's hearing, to take the call. His expression was sombre when he returned.

'Grab your jacket,' he said. 'Your parents have been found.'

Chapter 3 - *Inquest*

'Oh, babe, I'm so sorry.' Sadness in his girlfriend's voice. 'That's rough on you, it really is. Will there be an inquest?'

Matthew and Lauren were lying on his sofa, her arms around him. The pale June sunshine filtered through the windows, glinting off the glass doors of the wood-burning stove. Lauren's breasts pillowed his head, the musky scent of her skin drifting into his nostrils.

'Yes. A coroner's ruling is required, given the circumstances.'

'The police found your parents at Blackwater Lake, right?'

'Yeah. Didn't take them long, not when I told DS Hutton Dad worked there.'

'Any idea what happened?'

'Seems he smothered Mum with a pillow - the one he took from their bed.' Christ, how the hell had Joe Stanyer, who'd never shown any hint of violence, conceived such a notion? Only one answer to that. The man had been stretched beyond his endurance.

'Then Dad killed himself.' His voice cracked on the words.

'How did he die?'

'Drowned himself in the lake.' *Why didn't you talk to me, Dad?* More to the point, why hadn't

22

Matthew visited more often? He didn't think the crushing guilt would ever leave him.

Lauren seemed to sense his thoughts, not saying anything, simply hugging him tighter. DS Hutton had given him an account of what must have happened the night his parents died. His father, desperate, trapped, had chosen drastic measures. Unwilling to yield his wife to a care facility, he decided on a solution that would release Evie from the Alzheimer's turning her brain to Swiss cheese and spare him the torture of seeing the woman he loved destroyed by dementia. Her body, hidden by the nearby trees, was discovered by the fence that separated the public area from the private one at Blackwater Park. It seemed her husband drove her there at night in their ancient Toyota, abandoning the car at the entrance. A pillow from their bed and a flask of Johnny Walker accompanied him. He walked Evie to the lake, encouraging her to lie on the grass between the trees and the water. Then he smothered her with the pillow. A single red rose was found on her body.

Next, he'd deposited four house bricks into his clothing. He'd dressed for the occasion, wearing cargo trousers and a sweatshirt with large pockets. Despite being teetotal, he then drank enough whisky to inebriate a horse. The police lab found traces of Evie Stanyer's anti-anxiety medication in the dregs, his father having ground up her pills before mixing them into a flask of Johnny Walker. Once at Blackwater, he'd consumed the lot. Then he walked into the lake, wading out until his feet no longer touched the bottom. Its chilly embrace enfolded him as he sank under the water, the booze and tablets easing his death. After the police discovered Evie Stanyer's corpse, it didn't take long to locate her husband, not once divers searched the lake.

'Maybe you should go there.' Lauren's voice roused him from his reverie. 'To where they found the bodies, I mean. It might help you come to terms with their deaths.'

Why hadn't he thought of that?

'Will you come too?' He already knew what her answer would be.

*****

Despite the June sunshine, the wind sliced through Matthew, penetrating his thin jacket, whipping his hair from his brow. He stared at the thick line of Scots pines fringing the opposite shore of Blackwater Lake. Beside him stood Lauren, her arm tucked into his, her head resting on his shoulder.

At least ten years had passed since his last visit to the park. Not much had altered. The children's playground had changed colours, thanks to its periodic repainting, same as the cafe and gift shop. Blackwater Park was the Victorian seat of a local family, rich from the spoils of the tobacco trade. The area of Blackwater was named after them, but by the nineteen-fifties, their fortunes had dwindled. In the early sixties they remodelled the grounds, diverting the stream running through them into the nearest river. Scots pines were planted to conceal the house once the south side of the park was opened to the public, a cafe and gift shop being their plan for making money. The north side, where the family house stood, remained private, off limits. Decades later, the Blackwaters employed Joe Stanyer as groundsman for both areas.

'Have they said when the inquest will be?' Lauren asked.

'Next Tuesday. There's little doubt the verdict will be murder-suicide, from what DS Hutton told me.'

Christ, his head was a mess. His dominant emotion was still self-reproach. 'I've been such a lousy son. Hutton told me that was a form of survivor's guilt.' Matthew snorted. 'Yeah, right.'

'You're being too hard on yourself, babe.'

'Am I?'

'Yes. You couldn't have anticipated what your father was planning.'

'He was at the end of his tether, I know that much. Desperate people do desperate things.'

'You can't blame yourself. Your mother's dementia is what caused this. Her aggressive behaviour, her rapid deterioration. Your father must have been under one hell of a lot of strain.'

'Yes. He was.'

'You need to cut yourself some slack. Wait here. I'll be back in a minute.' With no further explanation, Lauren walked away, towards the picnic area. He watched her stride off, assuming she was going to fetch coffee, while mulling over her words. Maybe she had a point, but the guilt still gnawed away at him. Made a thousand times worse by the horror of identifying his parents' bodies. Supine on the morgue table, his mother had looked asleep, not dead, her expression peaceful at last. He'd reached out his hand, trailing it over her cheek. Her skin was dry under his fingers, like old cloth.

'I'm sorry, Mum,' he had whispered.

In contrast, his father's face had shocked him. Blackwater Lake had ravaged it, despite the best efforts of the morgue staff. Puffy, blotchy, Joe Stanyer's features bore testimony to the thirty hours he'd spent underwater. Matthew barely managed a hasty, 'That's my father,' before vomiting up his breakfast.

Back in the present, he watched as Lauren walked back towards him. In her hands, she held two pink roses.

'I saw these on the way in, growing near the picnic area,' she said. 'Didn't you tell me they were your mother's favourite flower?' Without waiting for an answer, she stepped closer to the water, tossing the two stems onto the water. The gesture moved him more than any words ever could.

*****

After the inquest a week later, Matthew and Lauren returned to her flat. The verdict was murder-suicide, just as the police had predicted. Not surprising, given his father's farewell note, but he felt flat, almost numb.

'You'll be selling the house, I take it?' Lauren asked.

'Guess so.' Not that he expected the place to fetch much, it being what estate agents dubbed 'suitable for DIY enthusiasts'. Living there himself might save on rent but held as much appeal as a rectal examination with a cactus. The house was a nightmare he'd escaped years ago. Crete was home, not Blackwater.

'Did either of them leave a will?'

Matthew doubted it. Would they have thought it necessary? As their only child, he stood to inherit everything anyway. Besides, if it existed, where the hell was it?

Later, back home after pleading the need for an early night alone, Matthew lay in bed, a headache pounding at his temples. To find his parents' wills, if they existed, he'd need to clear the rubbish that engulfed the house. Hell, he'd have to do it anyway if he intended to sell it. His mind baulked at the thought. Where the fuck did he start?

Most of it, he supposed, could be chucked without a backward glance. Even the homeless shelters wouldn't accept the food, most of it being years old. He'd hire a skip and heave all the tins of beans, every last can of tuna, into it, thus removing a good third of the hoard. Afterwards he'd move onto the toys and clothes. Nothing there a charity shop would want; everything was dirty and damaged. Another quarter gone. That left only boxes of books, papers and memorabilia. He'd have to sift through each item in case he found a will.

Matthew let out a breath. Soon the house would be free from the hoard's stranglehold. Then he'd get an army of cleaners to blitz through the dust and dirt, rip up the carpets, readying the place for sale. His decision made, relief rose to the surface, allowing the grief he'd been suppressing to swamp him. Tears blurred his eyes as memories of his mother flooded in. In one, her cheeks were flecked with flour, her sleeves pushed up, as she rolled pastry. He recalled her smile as she offered his six-year-old self a jam tart.

'Just the one,' she'd always say. 'Don't want to spoil your appetite.'

Uncomfortable with displays of emotion, Evie showed her love through the family's meals, cooking most from scratch and serving them in generous portions. As a child, Matthew's metabolism burned through her food faster than a Maserati. So did Joe's, given his eight hours a day of manual labour. Evie didn't follow suit, carrying several excess kilos of flab.

Small wonder she struggled with her weight. Besides her penchant for cooking, she avoided exercise, rarely leaving the house. Along with her rose garden, it formed her world. As a child, Matthew used to plead with her to take him to Blackwater Park, to the swings and seesaws. She always refused, a shuttered look clouding her face.

His mother's aversion to the park meant he got to spend time with his father, though; Joe would often take him to the play area at weekends. A good, solid man, his dad. Christ, if Matthew had been a better son, Joe might not have smothered his wife then waded into Blackwater Lake weighed down with bricks and booze.

The contents of his suicide note kept running through his mind. '*Son. Your mother and I can't go on this way. I'm doing what I believe is best. God knows we've not always done the right thing. I'm sorry. About everything.'*

Pain drummed inside his skull. What had his father, a man who always played by the rules, meant about not doing the right thing?

Chapter 4 - *Cuttings*

Lauren wrapped her arms around Matthew. 'You sure I can't help? Even if it's just making coffee?'

'Got to deal with this by myself, babe.' He hadn't shaken his shame about the hoard. The dust, the dirt, the downright ugliness. The rank smell, at its worst in the kitchen.

'You don't have to do this alone, Matt.'

'Yeah, I do. Call it a guy thing.'

'Why not use a house clearance team? They'll haul the crap to the dump, then scrub the place from top to bottom. Saving you time and effort.'

'That'll cost money. Which I don't have.'

'Sounds like you don't want anyone in the house. Sheesh, is it that awful?'

'Like you wouldn't believe. Everything piled to the ceiling, covered in decades of dust.'

Lauren laughed. 'Might be a body hidden in there.'

'Not funny.'

'Did you ever tackle your mother about the mess?'

'I did more than that. I tried to get rid of some of it. A long time ago.' Matthew's mind spun back through the years. The memory still troubled him. 'I was sixteen. It was the school holidays; Dad was at work, Mum had gone to the doctor. With her out of the way, I decided to clear the hallway. Slung the newspapers into the rubbish bin, cleared the old tins of food. Then Mum walked in on me. She went hysterical.'

He'd watched the shock fly into his mother's face, followed by fury. The only time he'd been afraid of her. She didn't lash out at him, but it was close. 'What have you done?' she screamed. 'Don't ever – *ever*, do you understand? – touch things that don't belong to you.' Her expression caused him to inch backwards, unsure why she'd reacted so strongly. 'You will replace everything. Now.'

The family's meal that evening had been a silent, tight-lipped affair; afterwards, Matthew retreated to his room. Downstairs, voices sounded, their tension apparent even if the words weren't. The rap of knuckles against his door startled him from his thoughts.

'Son? Can I come in?' Without waiting for an answer, his father opened the door.

He sat on Matthew's bed, his expression shuttered. 'Your mother's sorry she got so angry,' he said. 'But you have to understand. The way she likes to live – sure, it's different. But she's fragile. What she does – it helps her cope.'

'It's not normal, though.' Fierce resentment surged through him. 'Have you tried to stop her from hoarding?'

His father's eyes slid away; Matthew feared he might not reply. Then: 'She gets agitated if I discard anything. Believe me, son, it's easier to play along.'

A question burned Matthew's tongue. 'What caused it with her?'

He never got an answer. His dad stood up. 'Come downstairs, Matty. Your mother wants to give you a hug.'

Now, back in the present moment, Lauren nodded. 'Now's your chance to get rid of everything, then. Once and for all.'

*****

An hour later, standing in his parents' hallway, Matthew didn't regret not dragging Lauren along. The hoard loomed larger, more overwhelming, than he remembered. The skip he'd hired was parked outside. Once he'd cleared the hallway and stairs, carting the other junk to it would be much easier.

Today was Sunday; he'd begged a week off work to get the job done. Eight days to uncover his parents' wills, if they existed. He hoped to find more than that, though; part of him yearned to discover clues about his family history, much of which remained an enigma. He'd never known his paternal grandparents; Joe Stanyer's mother succumbed to cancer when he was fifteen, his father following with a fatal heart attack whilst still in his forties. Joe had just turned eighteen, inheriting the house mortgage-free. As for his mother's parents, Evie Stanyer always deflected his questions, changing the subject whenever he asked. His father didn't help, merely saying he'd never met them.

Matthew forced his mind back to the task ahead. Time to get to work on the boxes of books and stacks of newspapers clogging the hall and stairwell. He walked into the kitchen, intending to get some bin bags from under the sink, but stopped when he saw the smashed pane in the back door, the shards of glass puddled on the floor.

Shit. Someone had broken into the house since he'd last been there.

Well, good luck to them, he thought. Any thief would probably take one look at the hoard and leave. There was nothing worth stealing anyway. He walked through the house, checking if anything seemed out of place. Was it his imagination, or did some of the boxes in his parents' bedroom appear to have been opened, the dust on top of them disturbed? Or had he done that himself when last here?

Either way, he wasn't going to worry; he'd fix the damage, then get to work. Matthew found some old plywood in his father's shed and boarded up the window, then swept up the broken glass before starting on the hallway. He put the break-in out of his mind. Not worth bothering the police over something so trivial.

'Kids larking around, probably,' Lauren said when he told her about it later. Matthew shrugged. He'd pretty much come to the same conclusion.

Seven thirty a.m. the next day saw him clearing the back room. A task that required his full attention, seeing as many of the boxes contained paperwork. Others were full of Matthew's old toys: battered Ludo boards, broken model cars, crude wooden animals. The latter had been carved out of wood from the Scots pines fringing Blackwater Lake. He picked up a giraffe, running his fingers over the smooth legs, the long neck. He'd watched his father whittle it one evening.

'Helps me relax,' Joe had said as his knife shaped the wood. 'Better than a shrink any day.' Before long, he'd carved a rhino, hippo and lion as well, giving Matthew each one with a brief, 'For you, son.' Three words, encompassing a world of love. Emotion welling inside him, Matthew set the carved animals to one side, ready to take to his flat. One day he'd give them to his own kid.

He worked on, getting hot and sweaty, until late afternoon, by which time he'd cleared most of the junk in the room. As he opened boxes, tossed away rubbish, he suddenly had the sensation he was being watched. Ridiculous, of course. The grim task of clearing the hoard must be affecting his nerves, making him imagine things. He couldn't shake the feeling, though. Cursing at himself for being a fool, he stood up, turned around. And froze.

Someone was staring at him through the window. As soon as the person realised they'd been spotted, they ran off down the side of the house; the glimpse Matthew got was so brief he couldn't even be sure whether he'd seen a man or a woman. He sprinted into the hallway, tearing open the front door, intending to confront whomever it was, but they had already disappeared.

Strange, he thought. One of the neighbours, perhaps, come to nose around, gather material for coffee morning gossip. Except that on the right of the Stanyers' house lived an elderly man who was housebound, on the other side a young couple. Someone from farther afield, then. Most likely they wouldn't be back, given the embarrassment he or she must be feeling.

He felt jittery for the rest of the afternoon, though. Coming so soon after the break-in, the incident rattled him. When the time came to leave, he couldn't get out of the house fast enough.

*****

It was amazing what his mother had accumulated, Matthew thought the next day, as he opened boxes, sorted papers, filled bin bags with the rubbish from the living room. As he worked from the door towards the window, Matthew realised what he was finding was becoming increasingly personal. First came a box of old photo albums filled with childhood pictures. He flipped through them, seeing himself morph from a baby through his toddler years to secondary school. After that, the photos thinned out, unsurprisingly. As a teenager, he'd preferred to spend his free time away from the hoard, mooching at Blackwater Park.

Every Christmas and birthday card he'd sent his parents filled one box. Matthew fought back tears. He'd not known his mother was so sentimental.

He opened another. More photo albums, mostly containing old Polaroid snaps, many taken at Blackwater Park. From the photos his parents, younger versions of them, stared at him. In one his mother brandished a beer bottle towards the camera, her ring finger bare. Before her marriage, then. There were several Polaroids of them together, taken via the self-timer. Always outdoors, his parents sprawled on a blue tarpaulin. Paper plates, cheese, baguettes beside Evie. Beer and lager bottles everywhere. Strange. Joe and Evie Stanyer had always been teetotal, yet here they were, downing countless Pilsners.

Matthew gazed at his mother. She must have been nineteen or so, given that she hadn't yet married his father, but appeared older. Greasy blonde hair strained over her skull in a ponytail. Her face was pallid, gaunt. Dark smudges sat under her eyes. His father didn't fare much better. Thinner than the man Matthew remembered, and as pasty as his future wife. Both of them looked as though they'd not eaten a decent meal in days, despite the food beside Evie.

A couple of packets showed his parents with another female; Matthew guessed her age as nineteen, maybe twenty. A looker all right. Huge baby blues, framed by a cascade of copper-hued hair. Her raised arm sported a gold bracelet, studded with blue stones, nestling against her elbow. The unknown woman's face laughed at him as she sprawled on the tarpaulin, a bottle in her hand. Who she was, Matthew hadn't a clue. He flipped over the photos, hoping to find her name, but the backs were all blank.

He hauled several boxes of photos to the front door, ready to take when he left. The skip, the third he'd ordered, was full from the day's efforts. One more box to go, then he'd head home. He pulled the next one towards him, and opened it. Inside lay a manila folder. Beige, fat with paper. He flicked it open, revealing a stack of newspaper cuttings, the top one dated thirty-four years ago, from the *Bristol Evening Post*. 'Still no trace of missing woman,' the headline pronounced.

He read through the clipping. One year after her disappearance, the whereabouts of a local woman, Kerensa Price, remained unknown. Despite a re-enactment to jog the public's memory, no clues had surfaced. The rest of the cuttings all focused on the same topic. From the one he held in his hand, a face stared up at him; the picture was black and white, but Matthew knew the eyes would be blue, the hair a rich copper. Kerensa Price was the woman partying with his parents in the photos.

From what he read, she'd lived in Sneyd Park, one of the smarter parts of Bristol. That puzzled him. How would his parents, born and bred miles away in Blackwater, have known someone like her? Try as he might, he couldn't link the girl from the posh part of town with the beer-drinking couple from Blackwater, apart from through the photos.

Strange that neither of them had ever mentioned knowing her, given the publicity surrounding her disappearance. Intrigued, Matthew took the folder of cuttings to the front door, placing it with the boxes of photos destined for his flat. He'd peruse them more thoroughly later.

Chapter 5 - *Denial*

Matthew didn't return to the house the next day. With good reason; at ten o'clock that morning his parents' funerals took place at Bristol's Canford Crematorium. Besides him and Lauren, the only mourners were two members of the Blackwater family for whom his father had worked for so long. After the service, he watched the coffins slide backwards out of sight, his hand clutching Lauren's.

'I'm sorry,' he whispered in his head as his parents disappeared from view. 'For not being a better son.'

Matthew stood up, surveying the almost empty room as he did so. To his surprise, at the back of the crematorium sat a woman, one who hadn't been there before. Thin, straggly grey hair, a look of sickness about her. As she stood to leave, she glanced towards Matthew, her eyes meeting his.

Not that he got the chance to ask her who she was. As he moved towards her, the funeral celebrant accosted him, striking up a conversation. While they were chatting, Matthew watched the woman leave the crematorium.

His girlfriend had also spotted her. 'Any idea who that was?' she asked, after the celebrant had gone. 'Is she one of your parents' neighbours, do you think?'

Matthew shrugged. 'Probably. Listen, let's go to my place. I need to talk to you about something.'

Once back at his flat, Matthew brewed strong coffee for both of them, before sitting beside Lauren on the sofa. His girlfriend took a sip from her mug. 'So what's on your mind?'

Matthew hesitated. Where to begin? Sleep had eluded him the previous night. He'd lain awake, picturing his mother's pallid face as she brandished her beer bottle in the photos. The contrast between the teetotal couple who raised him and the beer-swilling pair on the blue tarpaulin bothered him. The I-don't-give-a-fuck expressions on their faces brought to mind the piss-heads staggering around Bristol's city centre on a Friday night. Mountain, molehill, Matthew chided himself. His parents used to get drunk. It wasn't a crime. They'd not killed anyone. So why did the photos disturb him so much?

Kerensa Price, that was the reason. Put together with the cuttings about her disappearance, the pictures of the missing woman with his parents raised unwelcome questions.

Lauren shrugged after he finished recounting his concerns about the boozing. 'So your mum and dad were once heavy drinkers. Hardly unusual at their age, is it?'

'Let me show you something.' The box of photos sat on the floor by the coffee table; Matthew opened it, taking out the first packet and extracting a picture of his parents with Kerensa. Then he picked up the folder of cuttings, flipping it open and placing it on Lauren's lap.

She stared at the photo, then back to the cuttings. 'It's definitely Kerensa Price with your parents. Did they ever mention knowing her?'

'Not even once. I'd have remembered that name.'

'That's strange. Have you found out anything else about her? Maybe through Google?'

Lauren had a point. Slamming down his empty coffee mug, Matthew strode into his bedroom, returning with his laptop. The cuttings told him the bare bones of Kerensa Price's life. Now he needed more. Time to do some digging.

A plethora of results came up, mostly from newspapers, reporting the years of police attempts to solve a cold case now frozen solid. The most recent was dated two months ago, entitled 'Dying Mother's Appeal'. Intrigued, he clicked on it, Lauren peering at the screen alongside him.

Kerensa's photo flashed up, together with one of her mother. The missing woman was still fresh-faced, forever twenty, her skin smooth, her copper hair shiny. In contrast, Hannah Price appeared to be in her nineties, despite the caption putting her at seventy-eight years of age. Canyons grooved their way between her nose and mouth, etching sorrow into her expression. Wrinkles furrowed her forehead and chin. Heavy bags hung under her eyes, emphasising their dullness; hollows carved themselves under her cheekbones. White hair, thin and flat, framed her face.

Matthew read how, after a lifetime of smoking, Hannah Price had succumbed to lung cancer. She was dying, her final wish to discover what happened to her daughter.

'It's eaten me away over the years, not knowing,' the article quoted her as saying. 'I realise there's little chance of my precious girl being alive. But if she's dead, I'd like to give her a decent funeral. I'll die in peace if I can do that.'

'Her grief must have consumed her every bit as much as the cancer in her lungs,' Lauren commented. 'What that poor woman must have suffered.'

Matthew agreed. Hannah Price's face was stamped with decades of grief. He continued scrolling through the Google search results, picking one headed, 'Mother reveals her heartache over missing daughter.' Recorded on the twentieth anniversary of Kerensa's disappearance, the video showed Hannah distraught, pleading for information.

'I'll never forgive myself for arguing with her that evening.' Her voice cracked with emotion. 'Silly stuff about how she needed to get a job, quit partying. I'd lost track of where she went at nights, who her friends were. Kerensa stormed out, saying she was fed up of being nagged. That was the last time I saw her alive.' A tear slid down her cheek. The video ended.

'God, that's sad,' Lauren said.

Matthew read the accompanying article. At first, Hannah Price didn't worry. When darkness fell, prickles of anxiety began. Not knowing who

Kerensa socialised with, she couldn't call her friends. At three a.m. she reported her daughter missing. Police scoured the area, deploying teams of tracker dogs across Sneyd Park and Clifton Downs; appeals went out for witnesses, but no solid leads emerged. Kerensa Price had vanished.

The article closed with background details concerning the Prices. Matthew read with a start how Kerensa had lived in Blackwater until she was sixteen, attending the same school as Evie. After her mother's divorce, the two of them went to live with Hannah's parents in Sneyd Park. Hannah Price still lived there now.

'So Kerensa grew up a mere quarter of a mile away from your mother, went to school with her as well,' Lauren said. 'That's how they knew each other.'

Matthew had been thinking the same thing. Something nagged at his brain. He was aware a piece of the puzzle eluded him.

Then he remembered. His mother's words: *Such beautiful hair, she had.*

In her photos, Kerensa Price sported a rich waterfall of copper, long and thick.

What else had his mother said? *She deserved everything she got.* To whom had she been referring? What did she mean when she hissed, *The little whore should have kept her legs shut*? Was the unthinkable possible? Were his parents involved in Kerensa Price's disappearance?

His girlfriend knew him too well. She must have felt him flinch, seen the tension tightening his lips as the awful thought flashed into his head. 'What's the matter? You've gone all pale.'

'Look at her hair.'

'It's gorgeous. But why is that important?'

Matthew told her what his mother had said. 'Probably the dementia talking,' Lauren said. 'I'm betting what your mum said was a product of her Alzheimer's, nothing more.'

'She made another comment that was strange, though. The first time I saw her after getting back from Crete.'

'What?'

'Something about how she and my father swore not to tell. That it wasn't right, how she couldn't get the image out of her head. She never did say what she meant.'

His girlfriend shrugged. 'Probably nothing at all. I went through all this with my grandmother. The weird comments, the aggressive behaviour.' She set down the photo and the file of cuttings. 'I'll make us more coffee.'

While Lauren was in the kitchen, Matthew sifted through his suspicions. His girlfriend was right. His parents involved in the disappearance of a young woman? No. Not just no, hell no. However hard he tried, he couldn't imagine his mother capable of such a thing. So why soil her memory this way? Better all round to put the whole thing out of his mind.

Chapter 6 - *Separation*

By four o'clock the next day, Matthew had cleared the bulk of the junk from the back bedroom. Two more boxes, he decided, then he'd call it quits for the day.

The next one contained greetings cards, kept in their envelopes, the tops of which were slit. The writing was neat, far removed from his mother's spider-like scrawl. He examined the postmarks, all of which were stamped from Bristol. Someone local, then.

He pulled out the first card. A sprig of holly met his gaze, along with the words 'Wishing You a Happy Christmas' embossed across the top. His fingers trailed over the gold print, a loose flake of glitter sticking to his skin. Inside he read:

'Evie, please get in touch. I miss you.' On the opposite side, underneath the cheery 'Season's Greetings!' was written, 'With love, Izzy'.

Matthew flipped the envelope, revealing a return name and address. Izzy Kemp, 41, Willow Gardens, Blackwater, near Bristol. A mere quarter of a mile away.

He opened more of the cards, all from the same sender. His mother had received them twice a year, every birthday and Christmas, for four years, starting before he was born. Never any clue as to Izzy Kemp's identity. Evie Stanyer had been an only child, with no surviving female relatives. He shrugged, slinging the cards back in the box, ready to take to a recycling bank later.

More photos in the next one, some black and white from decades ago; others were colour and more recent. Matthew flipped through them, not taking in what he was seeing at first. Two girls, the face of one announcing her to be eighteen, twenty at most; the other was a couple of years older. Mutual affection lit up their smiles. The hair of the older girl shone a dark honey, that of the younger a pale blonde. Same eyes, a similar upturn to the noses, identical fleshy lips. They were sisters, couldn't be anything else, and the flaxen-haired one was his mother.

Matthew's breath caught in his chest. The air in the room grew thick, cloying, as his mother's face, next to that of her sibling, smiled at him. He'd always believed her to be an only child. Not so, it seemed. Why had she never told him she'd had an older sister?

He selected another photo, this one black and white, its edges creased and worn. The sisters again, much younger, around ten and twelve, their smiles absent. Behind them stood a man and woman, presumably his grandparents. His mother told him a burst water pipe had destroyed all her photos of them. Why lie about such a thing?

He stared at the harsh faces of his grandparents. Rigid expressions, their mouths set, no compassion or love evident anywhere. Was that why their children appeared so cowed, so silent? So unlike the later photos?

Matthew glanced at his watch. Five o'clock. Time to go home and shower away all this weirdness; he couldn't process his thoughts right now. He closed the boxes, stacking them together so he could carry them to his car. They were coming with him.

*****

'Let me see those photos.' Lauren, sitting beside Matthew on his sofa later that evening, took the packet from him. His girlfriend stared at the image of Evie Stanyer, the smiling version, and said, 'They're sisters. Have to be,' thus confirming his own suspicions. She turned over the photo. Matthew had already checked all of them. Nothing written on a single one.

'Her name's Isabelle.' Lauren's words caught him off guard.

'What? How do you know that?'

She laughed. 'It's written on the packet, idiot. "Isabelle and me".'

Christ, how had he missed his mother's handwriting scrawled across the flap? A connection clicking into place in his brain, he reached into the other box he'd brought home, handing Lauren the cards from Izzy Kemp. She read a few, her brow furrowed.

'Izzy must be short for Isabelle. Was Kemp your mother's maiden name?'

'No. Webster.'

'So your aunt was married. She must have got hitched young.'

'Why didn't Mum tell me she had a sister?' Bitterness laced Matthew's voice. 'How come I didn't discover I had an aunt during the investigation into my parents' deaths?'

'Hey.' Lauren's hand rested on his clenched fist, her cool fingers soothing his anger. 'She must have had her reasons. And the police probably stopped probing once they realised it was a murder-suicide.'

'I suppose so.'

'Have you considered contacting your aunt?'

Matthew shook his head. 'The last card arrived nearly thirty years ago. She'll have moved since then.'

'She might still be in Bristol, though. Try searching an online phone directory.'

'Then what? How do I introduce myself to an aunt who doesn't know I exist?'

'She might be unaware of her sister's death, remember,' Lauren said. 'She deserves to know, don't you think?'

*****

At breakfast the next morning, Lauren licked her finger, using it to mop up the toast crumbs on her plate. 'Behave yourself whilst I'm away. And don't chicken out of contacting your aunt.'

His girlfriend was off to a yoga retreat in Glastonbury for a few days. Matthew realised how much he'd miss her. Right now he could use a little moral support, given his impending search for Izzy Kemp.

Once he'd kissed her goodbye, he went to his laptop. First he called up BT's online phone directory; his fingers shaking, he typed 'Kemp' into the name box and 'Bristol' as the location, before clicking on 'Search'.

Seven results, but no I. Kemps. Even if her phone listing was under her husband's initials, none of the addresses were 41, Willow Gardens. She'd probably moved, hardly surprising after so long. Or else her number might be ex-directory. Damn. How the hell was he going to find her?

At his parents' house later that morning, he pondered the matter as he carted boxes to the skip. Despite the proximity of Willow Gardens, an unannounced visit, assuming Izzy Kemp still lived there, would doubtless be a huge shock for her. A letter might prove the best way, at least at first.

He finished the back bedroom by eleven, then took an early lunch before tackling his parents' room. Which was when he struck gold. At the back of a drawer in his mother's dressing table, he found an old address book. He almost chucked it in the pile destined for the skip, before he realised what it was. Inside, the pages revealed a childish version of his mother's scrawl; a young girl's book, this, the names presumably school friends. At the front was the message, 'If lost, please return to Eve Webster', along with the Willow Gardens address, from where his aunt had posted the cards.

His fingers shaking, he flicked through the pages, finding 'Izzy and David Kemp', this time in his mother's adult handwriting, in the 'K' section. At an address in Bedminster, although the entry had been heavily scored through. Out of curiosity, he opened the 'W' section. At some point, Evie had crossed out 'The Websters', leaving only the Willow Gardens address and phone number. She'd also written a name beside it: Izzy.

Bingo. Maybe he'd get to speak to his aunt after all.

*****

By the time Matthew had finished for the day, only the furniture remained in the house. Still no sign of a will. Before leaving, he spent a few moments walking through each room. Amazing how much larger the place seemed without the stranglehold of the hoard. The air seemed lighter, clearer. So did he. As if by destroying the hoard, he'd broken the chains binding him to Blackwater. A return to Greece, Lauren at his side, was growing in appeal.

Before he left, Matthew tucked his mother's address book in his jacket pocket. He'd phone Izzy Kemp's number tonight, and pray she hadn't moved.

Chapter 7 - *Suspicion*

Matthew drove to 41 Willow Gardens the next day after lunch, his nerves stretched taut. His aunt and he had spoken on the phone the previous evening, a conversation rendering Izzy Webster, now using her maiden name, distraught with grief. The phone had rung for ages before his aunt had answered; Matthew got the impression she rarely received any calls. She'd been unaware she had a nephew and had only found out about his parents' deaths from neighbourhood gossip.

'I don't own a television. Or even a radio,' she'd sobbed. 'How else was I supposed to hear about Evie's murder? I don't even buy any of the newspapers.'

Once at Willow Gardens, he sat in his car, wondering about his aunt. What kind of person didn't own a television or radio, never read a newspaper? Was self-neglect his aunt's version of his mother's hoarding? Matthew took a deep breath. Only one way to find out.

He pushed open the gate, noting the rust, the flaking paint. Matched by the rotting windowsills, the weed-choked garden. His aunt clearly hadn't undertaken any maintenance in years. His fingers took hold of the knocker, gave it a firm rap.

When the door opened, Matthew's breath stilled in his chest. Standing before him was the woman he'd seen at his parents' funerals. Hard to equate her with the youthful Izzy of the photos. Time hadn't dealt kindly with her; she appeared a decade older than the fifty-seven years he thought she must be. Her figure was gaunt, incipient osteoporosis signalling itself in her neck and shoulders. Thin hair, its former honey colour now pale grey, straggled around her face. Sunken eyes gazed at him, their whites threaded with veins; the flesh of her cheeks was moulded to her skull. The resemblance to his mother still lurked in her nose and lips, however.

'Come in,' Izzy Webster said. 'I'll get us some coffee. Make yourself comfortable.' She gestured towards an open doorway.

Once inside, he glanced around. The room was plain to the point of austerity. As she'd said, no TV or radio. The walls lacked pictures, the paper yellowed and peeling. No ornaments graced the oak sideboard, no plants adorned the windowsills. The sofa on which he sat was hard, uncomfortable, a relic from a bygone era. He got the impression that nothing had changed in this house for decades.

Izzy returned with a tray complete with mugs and two slices of chocolate sponge. She handed Matthew his coffee and cake, before sitting opposite him in an armchair.

He was curious. 'Why didn't you introduce yourself at the funeral?'

She bit her lip. 'I didn't know who you were. I've been out of Evie's life since before you were born. And I'm not good with people I don't know.'

That made sense. 'I understand.'

'I can't believe you're here,' Izzy said. 'Or that I have a nephew.'

'I can't believe it either.'

'I always hoped—' Tears choked her voice. 'To be reconciled with Evie one day.'

What the hell could he say? 'You'd not seen her since her marriage?'

'Didn't even get an invitation. After she met your father, she cut me out of her life.' Bitterness filled her tone. Izzy Webster had clearly disliked her brother-in-law.

His aunt gazed at Matthew, her perusal intense. 'You're nothing like her. You favour your father.'

'So I'm told.' He stared back at her, struck by how haggard her face was.

'I look ill, don't I?' As he fumbled for something to say, Izzy pre-empted him. 'I'm dying.'

The words crashed over him. He cleared his throat. 'I'm sorry.'

'Don't be. I've not led a happy life. Won't be sorry to quit it.' She leaned closer. 'You'll be wanting to know. Everyone does, but few people have the guts to ask. Brain tumour, inoperable.'

Shit. The image of Hannah Price, dying from lung cancer, forced its way into his mind. Both women bore the stamp of imminent death in their features.

'Only got a few months left,' Izzy Webster said. 'Something else not many people ask. I've defied the doctors, staying here as long as I have. But I'll need hospice care before the year is out.'

As Matthew struggled to respond, his aunt said, 'Tell me about Evie. I need to know how she died. I want to hear the details from you, not my neighbour.'

He sucked in a lungful of air. It felt like a low blow to shovel more grief her way, but he had no option. Matthew set his coffee mug and his plate, now bereft of cake, on the table beside him. Then he told her. The bare facts, no more, about his mother's illness and his father's solution. When he finished, silence fell. His aunt's skin had grown paler, something he'd not thought possible. Tension tightened the muscles around her jaw, shadowed her eyes.

At last she spoke. 'I never liked Joe Stanyer. Did she have a good life, though? With him, I mean?'

'Yes. Devoted to each other, they were. That's why he did what he did.' He swallowed. 'So she wouldn't suffer any longer.'

His aunt smiled. For a second, it erased the exhaustion etched on her features. 'She was happy. That's wonderful. All I ever wanted was for Evie to escape her past.' She leaned forward, her smile gone. 'Let me tell you about our childhoods. So you'll understand.'

Matthew recalled the fear on the sisters' faces in the photos with his grandparents. Whatever Izzy revealed, it wouldn't be pretty.

'Back then we were Eve and Isabelle. We didn't call ourselves Evie and Izzy until after we left home. A way of rebelling, I guess, of escaping the formality with which we were raised. My parents were devout Christians. A local fundamentalist sect, now defunct. Church every Sunday, scripture classes, daily prayers. Everything revolved around sin, sacrilege and Satan. It never occurred to them that beating your kids black and blue for not reciting word-perfect passages from the Bible might be a sin.' Her laugh was devoid of mirth. 'Our whole childhoods were lived in terror of committing some misdemeanour. So many things were temptations from the devil, apparently. Television and radio, for example. Even now I can't bring myself to own either one. Pop music was also evil, along with alcohol and most of all sex. Evie was my friend, my ally, my only source of love, during those long miserable years.'

'I'm sorry.' The words seemed wholly inadequate.

'I was always the one who tried hardest to please them. To avoid their fury, the beatings. Didn't work, of course; they always found something to fault. But Evie – she didn't knuckle under so easily. As a result, she copped their anger far worse than I ever did.'

'You never told anyone? Social services didn't get involved?'

'Didn't think we'd be believed. To block it out, Evie started to drink when she turned thirteen. Hung around the streets with boys from Nailsea or Barrow Gurney. She'd come home late, reeking of alcohol. When she did, my father beat the shit out of her.' She shuddered. 'Didn't stop her, though. Booze was her coping mechanism.'

'What was yours?'

She shrugged. 'I kept my nose clean, did my best to stay out of trouble. Then I met David. We dated in secret, then married when I turned eighteen.'

Her husband. The reason the name Kemp appeared on the Christmas and birthday cards. 'Were you together for long?'

'Two years. By the time our parents were killed in a car crash, I'd already filed for divorce. I moved back here when Evie and I inherited the house.' She grimaced. 'Took cleaning jobs to get by. I've not had much of a life, really.'

'You never ran into Mum? What with both of you living in Blackwater?'

'God, no. I always avoided that area. It would have hurt too much to see her.' A hitch in her voice betrayed her emotion. 'These days I'm almost a recluse. The only time I leave the house is to go to the shops. Or to the hospital. I stayed close in case she ever needed me, though.'

'What happened with her? With the drinking?'

'It got heavier, over time. Besides the booze, Evie started sleeping around. It's a wonder she never got pregnant. Before she left home, the arguments with our parents worsened, especially after she met your father.'

'How did they meet?'

'Evie used to hook up with some local lads after school in Blackwater Park. They'd drink beer, hang out, have sex. Your father was working as a groundsman there. Seemed she fell for him hard. By then, she was stealing money from our parents to buy alcohol. The rows got worse. On her eighteenth birthday they changed the locks, screamed at her through the letterbox she was no longer their daughter. They were killed not long afterwards.'

Christ. His mother had endured one hell of a start to her life. It explained her reluctance to discuss her childhood.

'So what happened after they threw her out?'

'She went to live with your father. Not surprising, seeing as she spent most of her time at his place anyway. I visited a few times, before we became estranged. It was messy, beer bottles everywhere. From what Evie told me, Joe Stanyer turned to drink after his mother died from cancer. It's a wonder he kept his job, but I guess at that age it's easy to recover from a night of boozing.'

'Was there…' Matthew paused, unsure how to phrase his question. 'A lot of junk in the house?'

His aunt shook her head, puzzlement in her expression. 'No. Just the bottles. Why do you ask?'

He told her about the hoard. 'That's how I knew you existed. When I found the cards you sent. Along with the photos of you as girls.'

'Ah, those. I sneaked back after Evie told me they'd kicked her out. Found the pictures of us as kids, along with the rest of her belongings, in the garbage and gave them to her.' Her brow creased. 'What you say about the junk surprises me, though. Evie was never that way growing up. We weren't allowed many things, you see. Our parents told us it was sinful to want possessions.'

'Mum went to the other extreme, believe me. The hoard was my nightmare as a child. Made me feel she and Dad were weird.' Matthew shook his head. 'Strange, isn't it, how some people live?'

'It may not have been a lifestyle she chose, remember. Choice and compulsion don't always go together.'

'Guess I'll never know what sparked it. There's so much they didn't tell me.' Matthew failed to prevent bitterness seeping into his tone. He remembered Izzy's cards to her sister. 'Can I ask you something?'

'Go ahead.'

'What happened between you two? Why the rift?'

His aunt's expression grew pensive. She didn't answer at first, her fingers twisting in her lap. When she spoke, her tone was strained. 'Evie suffered jealousy issues. She became convinced I was making a play for Joe, despite the fact I didn't even like him.' Pain echoed in her voice. 'We had a huge row. She screamed at me to get the hell out of her life.'

Izzy's words came as a shock. He hadn't known his mother possessed a jealous streak.

Curiosity showed in his aunt's expression. 'Did you find any other photos of me in the hoard?'

'No. Unless they're in the boxes I've yet to check.'

'Evie must have destroyed them.' Her voice held an odd note. Sadness, he decided; her estrangement from her sister was still a raw wound, it seemed.

'We were so close once. But the drink – it changed her. She often became angry, aggressive. Their lack of money didn't help. Joe didn't make much at his job. Most of his wages went on booze. Neither of them was a full-blown alcoholic, but they certainly drank hard.'

'My parents were always teetotal. Something must have made them give up the drink.'

'Whatever it was, it happened round about the time we argued. A month afterwards, I went to their house when Joe was at work. I called Evie's name through the letterbox. If she was there, she didn't respond.'

'That must have hurt.'

'Like you wouldn't believe. I missed her so much. Before I left, I peered through a window. No beer bottles anywhere; I'd never seen the place so clean. A few boxes had appeared under the windowsill, though. Maybe that's when the hoarding started.'

Precipitated by the row with Izzy? His aunt's words confirmed something Matthew had been wondering about. The spot where he found the cuttings about the missing woman's disappearance probably represented the genesis of the hoard. But why had the cuttings been so important to his mother?

'I have another question. Does the name Kerensa Price mean anything to you?'

His aunt didn't answer at first. When he glanced at her, she appeared startled by the change of subject. 'No. Should it?'

'You're sure?'

'Never knew anyone by that name. Kerensa Price, you said? Doesn't ring a bell. Back then, Evie and Joe didn't have any friends besides me.'

'Doesn't matter.' He stood up. 'Listen, I should get going. Thanks for the coffee and cake.'

'You'll come again?' A plea in her voice.

'Yes.' It was the least he could do. Izzy Webster, terminally ill, deprived of her sister for decades, needed all the family she could get. Hell, so did he.

*****

Matthew sprawled on the floor under the windowsill in his living room, the wall hard against his back. Beside him lay the boxes containing the cuttings about Kerensa Price along with the photos of her with his parents. Possibilities ran through his head. Perhaps Kerensa ran away for some reason, didn't want to be found. Or suffered an accident. He dismissed the latter possibility. Had that happened, most likely her body would have been found long ago.

Or there could be a darker reason. She might have been murdered. The most plausible explanation, as far as Matthew could see, was that she'd been killed and her remains hidden somewhere.

Now that his aunt had laid bare his mother's painful past, ugly suspicions hammered on the inside of his skull, refusing to quit. He let out a breath, forcing his brain to run through the facts. Both his parents once had problems with booze, as well as being short of money. Evie was prone to anger and jealousy issues. The question was: how did Kerensa Price's disappearance fit the picture?

A possible scenario ran through his head. Kerensa, upset after arguing with her mother, heading for Blackwater Park to meet Joe and Evie. Friends Hannah Price hadn't known about. Then what? His parents had been desperate for money. Was robbery the motive? Or had his mother's jealousy been a factor?

Never been able to forgive myself... I swore not to tell. So did your father. It wasn't right, though. What we did. Can't get the image out of my head.

Had his mother lost control of her temper, resulting in Kerensa forfeiting her life?

She deserved everything she got. The little whore should have kept her legs shut.

Be quiet, Evie, for God's sake! His dad's sharpness with his wife had shocked Matthew at the time. Now an explanation presented itself. Had he been desperate to silence Evie's ramblings in case they revealed her part in a decades-old murder? *God knows we've not always done the right thing.* Had he been referring to Kerensa's death?

I'm doing what I believe is best. At the inquest the coroner interpreted Joe Stanyer's words as indicating a desire not to burden Matthew. Was the truth very different? Had his father intended to conceal Evie Stanyer's crime from her son?

Right when he thought the horror of his parents' deaths couldn't get any worse, it seemed he was wrong. Matthew's chest grew tight as he struggled to breathe, the implications of his suspicions ramming home to him. His mother may have committed murder, with his father an accomplice. Impossible, surely, for the loving parents he'd known to have done something so awful? Then he remembered their boozed-up faces staring at him from the photos, and he couldn't be certain of anything anymore.

*****

Matthew awoke with a start at two in the morning, having fallen asleep on his sofa. His neck hurt like hell; the rest of him was stiff and chilled. He dragged himself upright, his brain reverting to his deliberations of last night. By themselves, the cuttings and photos proved nothing, rendering it pointless to contact DS Hutton. His parents couldn't answer for their actions anyway. Besides, was it fair on Izzy Webster to drag this skeleton from its closet, given that she was terminally ill? Was there anything to be gained by unmasking his mother as a potential killer, when precious little evidence existed?

Yes, was the answer. How much time remained before Hannah Price's death denied her the answers she deserved?

His eyes fell on the boxes he'd brought from his parents' house. Some remained to be checked; he might as well do it now. He hauled himself to his feet, walking over to grab the top one. Sitting back on the floor, he reached into it; more packets of photos. As he grasped them, his fingers met cloth. Something was underneath.

Matthew set the photos aside, pulling out the object. A woman's shoulder bag, square, its blue silk embroidered with flowers. Only a few inches across, small enough to conceal beneath the photos. A hint of perfume drifted from it towards his nostrils. He rubbed his fingers over the bag, tracing the green of the stems, the pink of the petals. Not his mother's style. She'd favoured earthy colours. The vibrancy of this bag didn't match her tastes.

Matthew tugged the zipper across, taking out a small address book. A purse matching the bag was also inside. In it were a few coins, no notes. A library card nestled in the wallet section. He pulled it out, reading the name on the top.

Kerensa M. Price.

Matthew flung the purse down, his breath harsh and uneven. Shit. Holy crap. His mother possessed the handbag of the missing woman. In a nanosecond his suspicions of her involvement tripled, quadrupled. Not just her, but his father, too. Joe Stanyer's employment at the Blackwater estate meant he'd had access to shovels, would have known where to hide a body. Odds were both his parents were guilty in some measure.

Shit. For a moment, he pondered the idea of drawing a veil over the past. No reason why he shouldn't burn everything he'd found, pretend he'd never harboured such suspicions. That way his parents would remain the loving father and mother he'd always known, untainted by murder. The temptation flared in front of him, its lure undeniable. Yet deny it he did.

Matthew knew he'd never be able to stick his head in the sand about something so important. He needed to find out, one way or another, whether his mother had killed Kerensa Price, and if so, where the body was concealed. Without involving DS Hutton.

Chapter 8 - *Search*

A stiff breeze whipped Matthew's hair into peaks as he gazed out over Blackwater Lake the next evening. The rays of the summer sun, not far from setting, glinted sparkles off the water; from the picnic area a waft of smoke and frying onions reached his nostrils. On the opposite shore, the row of Scots pines stood, thick and impenetrable. He'd come here for answers, but would the lake supply them?

If his mother had killed Kerensa, her body must be buried in the park. It made sense, given Joe and Evie's drinking sessions here, his father's job as groundsman. But where? Impossible for her to be by the Blackwater family house. No chance of interring a corpse in the public area either; the disturbed earth would be a giveaway. One other possibility: her grave might be among the trees near where the police discovered his mother. He walked towards them until the dense brambles prevented him going any further. Oaks, not Scots pines, lined this side of the lake, the thick undergrowth between the trunks proving Kerensa couldn't be hidden here. Matthew doubted the area was any clearer at the time she disappeared; to bury her, his father would have needed to hack through the brambles. Granted, his job afforded him the necessary tools, but the task would have taken too long. Besides, the ground angled up towards the car park at almost forty-five degrees, making it less than ideal as a grave site. Wherever Kerensa Price's body lay, it wasn't here.

The only other possibility was Blackwater Lake itself. When the police divers found his father's body, they'd not taken long. If Kerensa was there, her body must be beyond their search area, which meant anywhere within most of the lake. Sure, he held diving qualifications; he could hunt for her remains amid Blackwater's depths. How the hell to do it without drawing attention to himself, though? The idea held danger, too. He'd need to dive solo, at night, and weeds choked much of the water. Safety concerns ruled it out as an option. If Kerensa lay on the lake bottom, she'd have to stay there. Perhaps some secrets shouldn't be uncovered.

*****

Later that night, sleep eluded Matthew; by three a.m. he gave up trying. The memory of his parents' boozy faces in the photos haunted his thoughts. He sat up in bed, swinging his feet onto the floor, making his way into the kitchen to brew some coffee. Mug in hand, he went to sit on his sofa, the box with the Polaroids from before his mum and dad's marriage beside him. His eyes trailed over the first photo. In the background, the waters of Blackwater Lake rippled, dark and deep. The photo must have been taken early evening; the sun shone low over the horizon. His gaze settled on the right of the shot, his attention captured by what he saw. Something blue intruded into the picture, a length of azure tubing he recognised. Only one thing at Blackwater fitted that description; the metal frame of the swings in the children's playground. The tubing was one of the struts as it disappeared into the concrete that anchored it.

For the strut to appear in the photo without the Scots pines being visible, it could only have been taken in one spot. From across the lake, in the area closed to the public. As the shoreline curved towards the Blackwater family house, it changed depth from a gentle slope to a sharp drop-off into the water. For safety reasons that part lay behind a fenced-off area, inaccessible to the public. When the Blackwaters created the park, they retained that section for their private use. His father, being groundsman for both parts, enjoyed access to it via a footpath that began by the fence. The path hugged the shoreline of the lake until it ended among the Scots pines opposite the playground.

Matthew had sometimes explored that route. The first time was during the school summer break, on a hot August afternoon spent avoiding the ever-growing hoard. His fourteen-year-old self was idling near the picnic area. His father, busy with his duties, hadn't known his son was there. Matthew had raised his hand to wave, but Joe had disappeared through the bushes. The start of the hidden path was narrow, concealed from public view by trees. A metal gate lay across its entrance, padlocked shut, a sign proclaiming no entrance to the public. Matthew doubted many people knew the path existed. When he judged his father was far enough ahead, he climbed over the gate and followed him. The track was dusty under his feet, its earth dry from the summer heat. He ended up amongst the Scots pines on the other shore, where the trail disappeared amongst them. As it curved towards the lake, concrete rather than earth slapped the soles of Matthew's shoes. When he glanced down, he realised he was standing on a culvert that fed into the water, allowing any run-off to drain away. From his vantage point, the public picnic area, along with the children's playground, was visible to his right across the lake. Opposite him lay the start of the path, behind the metal gate, near the oaks. Shielded as he was by the Scots pines, nobody in the picnic area could see him.

After a few times, Matthew didn't explore beyond the gate again. Too much risk of running into his father, who wouldn't be happy at his son trespassing. Besides, the path and where it led held nothing of interest to him. He'd forgotten it existed until today.

From what he remembered, thick undergrowth choked the grove of Scots pines, making it as inhospitable a grave site as the trees on the opposite shore. Not the culvert area though. The concrete on which he'd stood was flat, an ideal spot to spread a tarpaulin. His father knew of the access path, along with the screen the trees offered to a couple who wanted their own private party. They must have taken the photos from on top of the culvert.

Shit. He rubbed his jaw, wondering how he'd missed this. He searched through the rest of the Polaroids. In a few the playground strut was visible across the lake, in others it wasn't, depending on the angle of the shot, but Matthew felt certain. His parents had conducted their boozing sessions on the opposite shore, across from the main public area. A spot he'd overlooked as a potential hiding place for Kerensa Price's body. Impossible for her to be buried amongst the Scots pines, given the dense undergrowth, but what if she were concealed elsewhere? The culvert on which he'd once stood as a boy had served to drain run-off from the stream that used to run through Blackwater Park. No longer needed after the Blackwaters diverted its flow during the nineteen-sixties, but with no reason for its removal, it had remained there ever since, dry and disused.

A possible location for Kerensa Price's body. The only one, barring the lake itself.

Chapter 9 - *Discovery*

Light invaded Matthew's living room not long after five thirty a.m. He'd managed an hour, no more, of restless sleep curled up on his sofa. Time to get going.

He elected to walk the short distance, not wanting anyone to remember seeing his car at the park. What he was intending was shady, best kept covert. The place was deserted, it being too early for picnickers and most dog walkers. Once at Blackwater, he headed towards the path he'd explored as a teenager. Matthew slipped past the oak trees to where he recalled the metal gate being. Still there, its sign proclaiming the area off limits. He climbed over it, setting off along the path that skirted the lake, towards the Scots pines.

The undergrowth on the other shore was as dense as he remembered, apart from the path that culminated on top of the old culvert. Matthew stopped, imagining his parents' boozy nights here. Ahead of him lay much the same vista as he'd seen in the Polaroid snaps. Opposite where he stood were the struts of the children's swings, now painted green instead of blue, visible across the lake. No doubt remained in his head. This was the spot where his parents had taken the photos.

Matthew dropped to his knees, a foot from where the culvert ended. He drew in a deep breath, surveying the darkness of Blackwater Lake. Its waters had claimed his father's life. Might they also reveal how Kerensa's had ended?

He sprawled onto his belly, legs out behind him, his hands grasping the top of the concrete. Using his arms as levers, he propelled his head and chest over the water to peer inside.

The culvert was empty.

Shit. He'd been so sure. That'd teach him not to play amateur detective. He sat back on his heels, uncertain what to do next.

In his peripheral vision, something snagged his attention. A sliver of cord under the water, illuminated by the pale sunlight. When he edged closer to investigate, he saw it had been knotted around a root from one of the Scots pines, leading down into the blackness of the lake. His fingers reached out to tug the rope, meeting resistance. Its other end was attached to something that didn't yield easily. Matthew wrapped both hands around it, careful not to pull too hard. The rope felt frayed, rotten. He delved further into the icy water, meeting material. Plastic-like, with the pliability of cloth. Something hard he couldn't identify lay underneath. He dragged it upwards, still encountering resistance; the lower part seemed stuck. His efforts meant a few inches emerged, though. Whatever it was had been wrapped tight, bound with the cord, in a blue tarpaulin. Identical to the one he'd seen in the photos of his parents, on which they drank their evenings away. His hands explored the area under his fingertips, before he dropped the package with a cry of revulsion.

His breathing rapid and shallow, Matthew marshalled his thoughts. Had he found Kerensa Price? Unless the murder of someone else had also taken place at Blackwater Park, then the answer was yes. Now he understood the hardness he'd grasped through the tarpaulin. Her skull, of course. She was immersed vertically, feet down. In front of him the lake glinted darker in the morning light than it did a yard further out. Deeper, then, doubtless dug out when constructing the culvert. Kerensa Price's feet must be lodged in the dip, keeping her upright. Why attach her body to the tree root, though? Far easier to load the corpse with rocks and send it to the bottom of the lake. Then he recalled his father's suicide. He'd brought house bricks with which to drown himself, due to the lack of large stones in the park. Whoever had fastened the body to the root must have been afraid it might float and be discovered, so had taken the only option available.

Matthew gave another tug on the tarpaulin, the bottom of which remained stuck. He tried again. This time his efforts worked; the package rose to the surface amid a swirl of mud, the cord fastened to the tree root breaking free as it did so. The shock jettisoned Matthew backwards, causing him to curse. In front of him, the tarpaulin bobbed, its shape confirming the contents as a body.

The rational part of his brain urged him to contact the police, tell them what he'd found. Hell, didn't Hannah Price deserve that much? The problem was, he'd need to hand over the cuttings, photos and handbag, explain his reasons for going it alone. Chances were DS Hutton wouldn't look favourably on such actions. Besides, would linking his mother to Kerensa Price's death help anyone? A trial was impossible. Hannah Price could bury her daughter, sure, but what about Izzy Webster? Hadn't she suffered enough?

The wind whipped through the trees, a few drops of rain hitting his face. Matthew glanced at the sky. Ominous clouds now covered the sun; odds were a summer thunderstorm was imminent. Not a good idea to stay where he was, unless he fancied getting drenched. In front of him, the body in its blue tarpaulin edged across the water, moved by the breeze. That decided Matthew. He'd allow fate to take its course. If the storm broke, by mid-morning the tarpaulin might well reach the middle of the lake. Visible to everyone, including the new groundsman.

One thing to do first, though. He reached across, pulling the tarpaulin-wrapped corpse back towards him. Best to assume fingerprints might survive in water, in which case he needed to remove any he'd left. He fisted his hand into the sleeve of his jacket, then wiped where he'd touched before releasing the package into the lake. Kerensa Price's body inched further away as the wind gathered strength, the incipient storm peaking the water into soft ripples.

*****

A day later, news of the discovery of Kerensa Price's body dominated the media. Matthew was sitting with Lauren, back from her yoga retreat, watching the early evening bulletin at her flat.

'In breaking news tonight, the body of Kerensa Price, who disappeared from the Sneyd Park area of Bristol thirty-five years ago, has been discovered in Blackwater Park, a beauty spot close to the city. She was identified from her clothes along with her dental records.' The camera panned beyond the young female reporter to show the lake, with police investigators checking the culvert.

'To think they found her at Blackwater,' Lauren said. 'Isn't that weird?'

The reporter continued. 'The police are speculating that the motive for Kerensa's murder may have been robbery. Her handbag has not been recovered and a valuable gold and sapphire bracelet, given to Kerensa on her eighteenth birthday by her mother, is missing. She was wearing it on the night she disappeared.'

Christ. Matthew's mind flicked back to when he discovered the photos of his parents with Kerensa. Her raised arm, showing a bracelet studded with blue stones. Sapphires, from what the reporter had said. Did his mother kill her and afterwards rob the corpse? Then sell the spoils to buy booze? Revulsion, thick and bitter, clogged his throat. Where was the woman who raised him? Whom he'd loved? How could he reconcile his memories of Evie Stanyer with the fact she might have been a thief, a murderer?

'Look, they're interviewing the family,' Lauren said.

Next to the reporter was an older man, in his late sixties. She introduced him as Peter Moore, Hannah Price's brother. 'My sister has been through hell since Kerensa disappeared,' he said. 'She can now die in peace.'

'So sad,' Lauren murmured.

The reporter thanked him and turned to the camera. 'Hannah Price is terminally ill and has been appealing for information concerning her daughter's disappearance. The family have been desperate to locate her body so they can conduct a proper funeral. It remains to be seen whether her killer will ever be caught.'

*****

Over the ensuing week, Matthew watched every news bulletin he could. Fresh details emerged. The autopsy revealed Kerensa died from multiple stab wounds, suffered in a frenzied attack. Her ribs displayed blade marks, confirming the cause of death, as did her shredded clothes, although no flesh remained on the corpse. He'd assumed the tightly wrapped tarpaulin would keep the body dry, but water must have penetrated somehow, allowing decomposition. A good thing, he decided; any body fluids or hair left behind by his mother would have washed away or become unusable for DNA purposes.

With every bulletin, his tension eased. Nothing had been found to connect the murder-suicide of his parents to Kerensa's disappearance. Separate areas of the park, different circumstances, more than three decades between the two events. Case closed.

Chapter 10 - *Sample*

Matthew's mobile sounded, startling him into consciousness; he'd dozed off on his sofa. He grabbed his phone. Number withheld, so most likely a sales pitch. He swiped his finger over the screen. 'Matthew Stanyer.'

A deep male voice replied. No attempt to sell him car insurance, this. Instead, he found himself speaking with Detective Sergeant Paul Connelly from the Avon and Somerset Cold Case Review Team. Informing Matthew he needed to ask him a few questions in connection with the discovery of Kerensa Price's body.

'Shouldn't take long,' Connelly told him. 'Please understand, Mr Stanyer, you're not under suspicion in this matter.'

Panic engulfed Matthew nonetheless. 'I'm not sure how I can help you. I wasn't even born when this woman went missing.'

'I get that. However, we've found some links between Kerensa Price and your parents, Joe and Evie Stanyer. I'll explain more when we meet, but I'm hoping you can assist our investigation.'

Stay calm, Matthew told himself. 'Fine. When and where?'

'We can visit you at your home. If you prefer, Bridewell police station's an option.'

'Bridewell works better for me.' He didn't want cops here. Not with the possibility Lauren might drop by unannounced. Maybe he'd tell her later, once he'd spoken with the police. It depended how things went.

'Nine a.m. tomorrow good for you?' asked Connelly.

Within a minute, the call ended, leaving Matthew staring at his mobile. What the hell?

*****

'Sit down, Mr Stanyer.' Paul Connelly waved Matthew to a chair on the opposite side of the table. 'Can I get you something to drink?'

'Coffee, please. Milk, two sugars.' Matthew's mouth felt like the bottom of a hamster cage, his eyes gritty from lack of sleep. His nerves were stretched tighter than piano wire, his boss's irritation when Matthew phoned to plead a migraine having heightened his tension. Shit. As well as his employer, he'd need to lie to Connelly, the notion causing sweat to prickle against his shirt collar. The man was built like a wrestler, six four at least. Barrel chest, muscles straining against his shirt, thickly haired forearms. Pepper and salt hair, cropped short, framing eyes colder than Antarctic ice. A 'take no prisoners' expression in the set of his jaw. Everything suggested he wasn't a guy to piss off.

By the time DC Raynes, Connelly's subordinate, returned with Matthew's coffee, a few deep breaths had lessened his tension. Connelly was perusing the file in front of him, ignoring everything else. Raynes plonked a mug of tea next to his boss.

'Strong and sweet, just the way you like it,' he said.

Connelly took a sip before setting the mug aside, his action brisk. He clasped his hands, his forearms resting on the table. Beside him, DC Raynes held a pad and pen. Connelly cleared his throat.

'Thank you for agreeing to meet us, Mr Stanyer. As I mentioned when we spoke on the phone, I'd like to ask you a few questions in connection with the disappearance and murder of Kerensa Price. More specifically, to what extent your parents were in contact with Ms Price at the time of her death. As I explained, you're not under suspicion in this matter.'

Matthew fought to steady his voice. 'I don't think I can help you. As I said yesterday, I wasn't even born then.'

'I realise that. However, the discovery of Ms Price's body was the breakthrough we needed. I got talking to Detective Sergeant Hutton about the case. He gave me your mobile number after mentioning your parents' deaths at Blackwater Lake. My condolences for your loss.'

Matthew didn't reply, anxiety still tightening his chest. He took a mouthful of coffee, its sugary heat easing his tension.

'Until I spoke with Hutton, I didn't think there'd be any link between a recent murder-suicide and a thirty-five-year-old homicide,' Connelly continued. 'Back then, the team working the case checked into Ms Price's old connections, but Evie Webster wasn't even questioned. Not surprising, seeing how it appeared they were no longer in contact. Notes in the files indicate Kerensa attended Blackwater Girls' School, however.'

'So did my mother. Until she was eighteen.'

'Kerensa left at sixteen, though, when she moved to Sneyd Park. Mr Stanyer, to the best of your knowledge, did the two of them keep in touch?'

Matthew shrugged. 'No idea.'

'Your mother didn't tell you they were at school together? In the same class?'

'Mum never mentioned this woman.'

Connelly looked thoughtful. 'DS Hutton said she was a compulsive hoarder. That you got landed with one hell of a mess after your parents died.'

The memory of the dust, the dirt, the sheer awfulness of those dark rooms, choked with junk, forced its way into Matthew's head. 'That's an understatement. She'd been hoarding for over thirty years.'

'Did you find anything relating to Kerensa Price? Christmas cards, letters? Photographs?'

Matthew eyeballed the man full-on. 'No. Nothing at all.'

Connelly grimaced. 'I was afraid of that. Still, no harm in asking.'

'What makes you think my mother knew Ms Price at the time of her disappearance?'

'Just making enquiries, Mr Stanyer. When Kerensa went missing, nobody considered it worthwhile to question your mother. A four-year gap since Kerensa moved away, no obvious connection.' Connelly leaned forward. 'Now we're not so sure.'

'What do you mean?'

'Back then, we had no knowledge of any link between Kerensa and your parents. After my discussion with Hutton, that changed, once I discovered Evie Stanyer had been Kerensa's classmate. In the interests of investigating every possible angle, I decided to dig deeper. Which led me to check into your father's background. When I did, a couple of interesting facts presented themselves. One being that when Kerensa went missing, Joe Stanyer owned a dark blue Ford Escort.'

Matthew shook his head. 'Sorry. I wouldn't know.'

'Hannah Price saw her daughter get into a similar car that night. Navy in colour, she thought. Mrs Price didn't notice the make, model or registration number, though. She said a man was driving, with a female passenger.'

'Was she able to describe the occupants?'

'Not enough to provide a photo-fit. Young, white, that's all she remembered.' Connelly took a sip of his coffee. 'Another thing. Your father was charged as a juvenile with knife crime. Were you aware of that?'

'No way.' Matthew was flabbergasted.

'Seems he went off the rails after his mother died of cancer. Threatened someone with a knife after he'd been drinking. Got let off with a caution.'

Matthew shook his head. 'I had no idea. Not something he'd admit, I guess.'

'Probably not.' Connelly leaned forward. 'We need to eliminate him as a suspect, however.'

Fear nibbled at the back of Matthew's skull. He'd never considered his father might have murdered Kerensa. What possible motive could he have had? As he struggled for a reply, Connelly resumed speaking.

'How much of your parents' stuff have you cleared?'

A weird question, Matthew thought. 'Just a couple of boxes left to sort, and I've got those at home. The cleaners are coming in next week. I'll put the place up for sale as soon as possible.'

'I see.' Connelly leaned back in his seat. 'You've disposed of most of the contents, then?'

'Apart from the furniture, yes. Mum was a typical hoarder. Tinned food, newspapers, books. Filthy, damaged, of no use to anyone.'

'Did you keep any of your father's things? Clothes, personal effects?'

Connelly's question threw Matthew even further off base. 'No. Dad didn't have many clothes. I ditched those he owned. Dirty, full of holes.'

'Toothbrush? Comb? Razor?'

'All thrown in the skip. He kept loads of stuff, sure, but it was pure junk.'

'Don't chuck anything else away. And hold off on getting the cleaners in. I take it that won't be a problem?'

Matthew wiped his sweaty palms on his jeans. 'No.'

'One more thing.' Connelly leaned forward, eyeballing him. 'Kerensa's body had been immersed in water for thirty-five years. Despite what you see on TV crime shows, DNA degrades, doesn't always keep. The lake was cold, though, shaded by trees. The tarpaulin kept out sunlight and air, although a small rip allowed water in, meaning any flesh had long since decomposed. We've been working to extract DNA from the bones, however, and the lab's obtained a usable sample. Now we need a specimen of yours.'

Shock gripped Matthew. 'Why?'

'Can't tell you that, Mr Stanyer. Not at this stage of our investigation.'

'You want a link to my father's DNA.' Matthew's throat grew dry. The man's previous questions made sense now. He'd been after Joe Stanyer's skin cells, hair or saliva.

Connelly continued as though he'd not heard him. 'A simple mouth swab will suffice.'

Shit. He knew squat about how the police operated in such matters, but he didn't doubt Connelly possessed powers to demand a sample should he refuse. Even take it by force if necessary. The best option was to agree.

'I'd be happy to provide a swab if you think it might help. Listen, can we take a break? I need a piss.'

*****

Matthew selected a urinal and unzipped his fly whilst forcing air into his constricted lungs. Connelly's words echoed in his head. *We've been working to extract DNA from the bones.* What the hell was the man driving at? Kerensa Price had already been identified from her clothes and dental records. Why would the police need DNA from her bones?

He took a leak, then zipped up his fly and washed his hands, leaning against the basin. The porcelain lay cool against his arms as he pondered Connelly's words.

The lab's obtained a usable sample. For what purpose?

The answer flashed into his head. Only one explanation fitted. Connelly hadn't been talking about Kerensa's bones, but those of her unborn child. She must have been pregnant when she died, the foetus's skeleton discovered during the autopsy. In asking for his DNA, Connelly aimed to establish whether Joe Stanyer had fathered her baby.

The world around Matthew ceased to exist as he contemplated the goddamn irony of the situation. He'd always wanted a brother or sister. Trouble was, his half-sibling was as cold and still as Blackwater Lake.

Upon his return to the interview room, he didn't bother sitting down.

'Kerensa Price was pregnant, wasn't she?' He looked straight at Connelly. 'That's what this is about. You think my father might have been responsible.'

Connelly didn't confirm or deny Matthew's assertion. Not with words, anyway. For a nanosecond, though, his expression changed. Beside him, Raynes coughed, averting his eyes. Then Connelly's countenance morphed back into neutral.

'Like I said, Mr Stanyer, I can't provide details of an ongoing investigation. We appreciate your cooperation, though.'

Chapter 11 - *Results*

Surprise sounded in Izzy Webster's voice at the other end of the phone. 'Is everything all right? Has something happened?'

'Yes. Look, it's complicated. Lauren's out with friends, so I have a free evening. Can I come over?' Matthew needed someone with whom to discuss this latest turn of events, and his girlfriend wasn't an option. Best not to involve Lauren in any of this until he was certain his parents were involved in the murder of Kerensa Price.

Silence for a while. Then: 'Sure. Does seven o'clock suit you?'

*****

'Coffee?' Izzy appeared tired, drained, her skin the colour of old paper. He regretted springing this on his aunt, but what choice did he have? Not easy to tell a dying woman the police were investigating her dead brother-in-law as a murder suspect, but she deserved the truth.

'Please.'

'Milk, two sugars, right? I'll get the kettle on.'

Once Izzy returned with two steaming mugs, they retreated to her sofa. Matthew sipped his drink before setting it on the coffee table.

'Remember how, when I last visited, I asked you whether the name of Kerensa Price rang a bell?'

His aunt didn't reply at first. Then: 'Yes. I didn't recall who she was then, but I do now. It's been all over the news lately, so my neighbour said. Not having a television or radio, I don't keep up with such things. They found her body in Blackwater Lake, didn't they? Poor girl.'

'That's her. She's been missing for thirty-five years.'

'She went to the same school Evie and I attended. I was two years ahead of them, though, and close as we were, I didn't know all her friends.'

'They resumed contact again just before Kerensa's death.'

Izzy Webster stared at him. 'What makes you say that?'

Crunch time. Matthew told her about the cuttings, the photos, Kerensa's handbag and purse. The phone call from Connelly.

'Seems he's flagged up links between my mother and Kerensa. Along with the car Dad was driving back then. Hannah Price said her daughter got into a similar vehicle, one with a young white male and female in it. Once Connelly read in the file Mum and Kerensa went to school together, he asked me if I had any information.'

'Why? You weren't even born.'

'He thought I might have discovered something in the hoard. I lied, didn't mention the cuttings or photos. By themselves, they mean nothing. As for the handbag and purse, I can't explain Mum having those.'

'There might be an innocent reason. Perhaps Kerensa left them in their house by accident.'

Matthew frowned. A possibility, he supposed. 'He's on to something, though. Asked me to provide a DNA sample.'

'What? But why?' Shock echoed in Izzy's words. 'Unless—' She cleared her throat. 'I get it. The police suspect Joe Stanyer might have fathered her baby. They need DNA from a close relative to confirm or deny their theory.'

'Got it in one. There's little doubt the results will show Kerensa Price was pregnant with my half-brother or sister.'

His aunt shook her head. 'You're jumping to conclusions. You don't know what the DNA testing will reveal. Odds are the child wasn't Joe's.'

'What about Mum's jealousy issues? Maybe she stabbed Kerensa in a fit of anger because Dad fathered her baby.'

'Matthew.' Izzy's voice was firm. 'Your mother had her problems. But Evie wasn't a killer. Don't ever think that.'

'I don't want to. I can't be certain, though. Of anything. What if Dad killed her? Connelly told me he'd once been charged with knife crime. Maybe he feared being stung for child support payments. Or else he stabbed her, then stole her bracelet, the one that's missing.'

'Do you believe he'd do such a thing?'

'Not the man who raised me, no. But the people my parents were back then – anything's possible. You never liked him. Why?'

His aunt hesitated before answering. Then: 'Evie told me about the knife crime charge. His temper, the drinking – your father scared me, Matthew.'

So his father had inspired terror in Izzy. On top of the revelations from the police, Matthew's world was being shaken to the core. How could he equate the man who'd lovingly carved those wooden animals with the hard-drinking hothead described by his aunt?

*****

Two days later Matthew was busy with the quarterly stock-take of fins, masks and tanks at the dive shop where he worked. A mundane job, one that failed to keep his mind off his dead half-sibling. Once the forensics lab proved the genetic link with Kerensa's baby, Connelly or Raynes would call him. The questions about his parents would intensify. A cause for concern, given the box of photos, the file of cuttings and Kerensa's handbag were still at his flat. Should he move them back to his parents' house? Or even burn them? Otherwise he'd risk investigation for withholding evidence, not a scenario he cared to contemplate. But destroying evidence was far worse. Try as he might, Matthew couldn't reconcile the latter option with his conscience.

The police would interview everyone connected with his parents, of course, not just him. Not that the list would be long: his father's employers, Izzy Webster. Might be a while before a return to Crete was possible, though.

He'd broached the subject with Lauren last night; they'd been at her place, in bed. For once, Matthew hadn't been in the mood to make love; his head was preoccupied with DNA, Connelly, bones in a pathology lab. Instead, he'd lain there, wondering how to broach what was on his mind.

Beside him, Lauren poked his ribs. His girlfriend was as sharp as smashed glass; right now she was clearly aware he'd been brooding. 'Are you going to tell me what's crawled up your butt and died? Something's bothering you, isn't it?'

After six months together, he recognised the terrier in Lauren. No way would she let this go. Best to tell her. Some of it, anyway.

He didn't mention the cuttings, the photos of Kerensa, her handbag and purse. Instead, he told her about the phone call from Connelly, his visit to Bridewell, giving a DNA sample. His certainty that Kerensa Price had been pregnant with his half-sibling.

When he finished, Lauren blew out a soft whistle. 'Shit, babe. Why didn't you tell me before?'

Matthew shrugged. Good question. 'Wasn't sure how you'd react.'

She pulled him close, her arms offering comfort. 'What do the police hope to accomplish, though? Even if your father got Kerensa Price pregnant, it doesn't mean he killed her. Or that your mother did. There won't be a prosecution, so what's the point?'

'Hannah Price, remember. She's waited thirty-five years to get answers as to what happened to her daughter.'

'I guess. But it's all so woolly, isn't it? You can't even be sure Kerensa Price was pregnant. Or that it was your father's child.'

'Why else would the police need his DNA? Which they can't get, so they took mine instead.'

'How long until you find out?'

'No idea. I'm waiting to hear from them.'

He pulled back, gazing into Lauren's face. One he could picture beside him in Crete. They could make a life together, away from Blackwater. Drink ouzo, eat moussaka, dive in the Aegean Sea. Lauren could open an art studio. Tempt the locals with her pies. This woman been a rock in his life, right when he'd needed one, and for that he loved her.

'Listen, babe. How'd you feel about coming to live in Greece with me? When this is over?'

*****

As Matthew continued with the stock take the next day, his mind replayed her response. Lauren had been enthusiastic. They'd lain for hours hatching plans: a dive school for him, an art gallery for her, once the money from the house sale came through. The future looked promising. Afterwards they made love, the sex heated and urgent this time. Sated, his brain and body exhausted, Matthew fell asleep, Connelly and the DNA test far from his thoughts. Now, here at work among the boxes of snorkel tubes, his optimism returned. Somehow he'd deal with this.

The ringing of his mobile jolted him from his reverie. Private number. Could be Connelly, calling with news.

'Mr Stanyer? Detective Constable Raynes here.'

Matthew collected his wits. No reason Connelly shouldn't get his grunt man to confirm the paternity of Kerensa's child.

'Mr Stanyer, I'm ringing to tell you we are no longer pursuing our enquiries regarding your parents.'

Shock hit Matthew. Whatever he'd been expecting, it wasn't that.

'We've tested the DNA you supplied. Joseph and Evie Stanyer are no longer of interest to us in the matter of Kerensa Price's murder.'

'Then—' Matthew held his breath. 'Someone else fathered her baby?'

'Yes.' Raynes must have realised he'd confirmed Kerensa had been pregnant. 'I mean – yes, we have no more questions for you. Nothing indicates Joseph and Evie Stanyer were in contact with Kerensa Price at the time of her disappearance. Sergeant Connelly asked me to thank you for your cooperation.'

*****

Later that evening, at his flat, Matthew cradled a can of beer whilst chewing over what Raynes had told him. Joe Stanyer hadn't fathered Kerensa's baby. The police didn't consider his parents as suspects in her death.

Had he got it wrong? Twisted the facts into something they weren't? The file of cuttings must have been Evie's interest in a local disappearance, nothing more. The tarpaulin, the rope – such things were common as muck. Lots of people used tarpaulins – builders, fishermen, etc. – and carrying rope in a car boot was standard in case of needing a tow. He couldn't explain the handbag and purse, but perhaps his aunt was right; Kerensa had left them behind after a boozy drinking session. His mother's ramblings? Had to be the products of a diseased brain, rather than anything sinister. The truth was, he'd jumped to conclusions.

Once he finished his beer, Matthew remembered he still needed to check some of the boxes he'd taken from the house. They were piled by the coffee table, reminding him it wouldn't take long to sort through them. He glanced at his watch. Nine p.m. No time like the present, as Lauren was fond of saying. He crossed the floor to kneel beside them, opening the top one. More photos, still in their packets. He took out the first envelope, pulling out the contents.

At first he didn't comprehend their significance. More shots of his parents, boozing it up with Kerensa Price. Then: what the hell?

There, on the familiar blue tarpaulin, sat his parents. Beside them sprawled Kerensa. What he'd not anticipated was the woman sitting next to her.

His aunt, Izzy Webster.

Her words catapulted themselves into his brain. *Never knew anyone by that name. Kerensa Price, you said? Doesn't ring a bell. Back then, Evie and Joe didn't have any friends besides me.*

Yet here she was, sitting so close to the murdered woman they almost touched. Kerensa was an uncommon name, not easily forgotten. His aunt had lied to him. Something else flashed into his brain. His conversation a few nights back with her.

I get it. The police suspect Joe Stanyer might have fathered her baby.

The police hadn't made public Kerensa Price's pregnancy. If not for Connelly's expression and Raynes's slip of the tongue, Matthew wouldn't have known. Izzy Webster had, though. How? The police's reason for requiring the DNA sample wasn't something anyone would figure out straight away whilst in the middle of a conversation. It had taken him a while, but not Izzy. Her words had held certainty, too. She'd known about the baby when she shouldn't have.

He flipped through the rest of the photos. More of the same, showing Joe, Evie, Kerensa and Izzy in various poses.

His aunt's words, the first time they met: *Did you find any other photos of me in the hoard?*

No. Unless they're in the boxes I've yet to check.

Evie must have destroyed them.

Not sadness he'd detected in her voice, but relief. She'd been afraid he'd find these photos. Had she been the person who smashed the kitchen window before breaking into the house?

Izzy Webster had lied to him, and he intended to discover why.

Chapter 12 - *Bereft*

The following evening, Matthew stood outside Izzy Webster's house, his hands shoved in his pockets, the left one closed over the packet of photos. With shaking fingers, he pressed the buzzer.

Seconds later, his aunt opened the door. Her face was pale, her lips dry and cracked. The hollows of her cheeks had grown deeper since his last visit. When she spoke, however, her voice was warm. 'Matthew! What a lovely surprise.' She stood back to let him pass. 'I'll get the kettle on.'

He walked into the living room, turning to face her. 'I don't want anything to drink.'

Izzy Webster's smile faded. 'You seem upset. Have you heard from the police about the DNA test?'

Matthew took a seat in an armchair. His aunt sat on the sofa, concern in her expression.

'Talk to me. What's wrong?'

He cleared his throat. 'DC Raynes called me. Dad didn't father Kerensa Price's baby.'

Izzy Webster laughed. 'But that's great! Isn't it? Joe Stanyer had his faults, but he loved Evie. He'd never cheat on her.'

'It seems not.'

'So why the serious face? Isn't this good news?'

Matthew's fingers curled again around the photos. He brought out the packet, passing it to her. 'You lied to me.'

'Lied to you? No. What on earth—' As she spoke, his aunt flipped open the envelope, drawing out the photos. Her gaze fell on the top one, showing Joe, Evie, Izzy and Kerensa on the blue tarpaulin at Blackwater Lake. Her breathing hitched. As though mesmerised, she examined each photo, scrutinising it, tracing her fingers across the surface.

'You knew Kerensa Price at the time of her death. Yet you told me you didn't remember her.'

His aunt set the photos in her lap, casting a last look at them. 'I didn't lie. I forgot.'

'Your sister's friend? A woman with such a distinctive name? Whose disappearance was publicised all over Bristol?' Matthew's tone grew sharp. 'You're asking me to believe you didn't remember her?'

'Yes. It's the tumour, you see. My memory's not great anymore. You have to understand—'

'What about the baby?'

'What do you mean?'

'Kerensa's child. The police haven't made that public knowledge. There's no way for you to have known. Yet you did.'

'I… I guessed she must have been pregnant. Why else would they need your DNA?'

'You're lying.' Ice in Matthew's tone. 'Took me a while to figure out their reasons. You, though

– you didn't need two seconds. Why? Because you already knew Kerensa was pregnant.'

'No, I swear—' A gasp tore from her mouth as Matthew closed the gap between them, grabbing her shoulders. 'Don't! You're hurting me—'

'Did you break into my parents' house after they died? To search for those photos?'

'No! Of course not. I don't know what you're talking about.'

Ice turned to steel. 'What happened? Who killed Kerensa Price?'

'Let go, you're bruising me—'

'Tell me the truth. You owe me that much.'

She wrenched away, her lips twisted and angry. The photos slid from her lap onto the floor. 'You want the truth? Fine, I'll tell you. But you won't like it.'

'Try me.'

'It was your father, OK? Joe Stanyer killed Kerensa.'

Matthew sat back, stunned. 'But why? He didn't get her pregnant.'

'True, but Evie believed otherwise. Her jealous accusations were what set him off. He had a temper on him, and back then it flared up a lot, what with the drink and his money worries. Evie phoned me, told me what happened. Hysterical, she was. One night the three of them were partying at Blackwater, the part where the public weren't allowed. A row broke out. Kerensa taunted Evie, told her the baby was Joe's. Evie was obsessively jealous where he was concerned. She always suspected Kerensa was after Joe.'

'Was she?'

'No, but the little madam enjoyed stirring up trouble. Anyway, Joe denied it. Flew into one of his rages, made worse by the drink. He pulled out a knife and stabbed Kerensa, over and over. Stomach, chest, everywhere. Like a madman, Evie said, even though she tried to pull him off.' Her voice shook.

Matthew attempted to process Izzy Webster's words. 'What about the bracelet?'

'Kerensa's sapphire one? He must have stolen it from her body. I'm guessing he sold it for beer money.'

'No.' Matthew shook his head. 'My father wouldn't have murdered a pregnant woman.'

'You're wrong. You've no idea what he was capable of back then.'

'Maybe not. But the man who raised me didn't have a temper.'

'He was always on the beer in those days. Alcohol screws people up. It did your father.'

'So he killed her, then disposed of the body in Blackwater Lake?'

'Yes.'

'No.' Matthew shook his head. 'I can't believe it. I won't.'

It was hard for him to accept, even factoring in the alcohol. Despite his reluctance, his aunt's words sounded in his head. *His temper, the drinking – your father scared me, Matthew.* Then there was Joe's knife crime conviction to add to the picture.

'The next morning, I went to the house after he left for work,' Izzy continued. 'Evie was distraught. She'd convinced herself Kerensa was to blame. Said she was a little whore, how she deserved everything she got.'

His mother's words. Cognitive dissonance at its finest, lending credibility to his aunt's revelation.

'I visited her every day after that. Needed to, for my peace of mind. I tried to avoid seeing Joe, but sometimes he came home early. I never spoke to him, couldn't look him in the eye. That's what sparked Evie's jealousy. Why she broke off contact with me.'

'I don't understand.'

'She believed I was avoiding Joe through guilt. Because I secretly loved him. Ridiculous. I loathed him, was frightened of him, but she insisted I was lying. One day she screamed at me, telling me she knew my dirty little secret, how I was no sister to her. Said she hated me, how she never wanted to see me again.' Izzy wiped her eyes with the sleeve of her blouse.

Matthew fell silent, processing his aunt's words. Her face was paper-pale, the emotion in it unmistakable.

'I'm sorry I lied. I couldn't tell you, you see. Didn't see the point. It all happened so long ago, and Evie swore me to secrecy. I urged her to turn your father in to the police, but she wouldn't.'

'Why not?'

'Because of you.'

Matthew stared at her. 'What do you mean?'

'Evie had found out she was pregnant. She was screwed up, remember, the child of abusive parents. All she wanted was the happy family scenario, the one denied her as a kid. Impossible with Joe in prison for murder.'

'You said—' He swallowed. 'That you hadn't known about me.'

'I didn't, not the details. By the time she gave birth, she'd cut all ties between us. I lied to protect you, Matthew. From the truth about your dad.'

Yes. He understood that. She'd not wanted to burden a son with the sins of his father.

'I'm sorry,' Izzy said. 'Do you blame me?'

'No. You were between a rock and a hard place, as they say.'

His aunt stood up. 'This must be difficult for you. We could both use more coffee, I think. I'll get us some cake as well.'

*****

Matthew headed upstairs, in need of the bathroom, trying to order his thoughts. His father had been a murderer, his mother complicit in concealing the crime. One hell of a painful truth to swallow, coming so soon after their deaths. He'd have to do the right thing, tell Connelly, give Hannah Price the closure she deserved, but God, where would he find the words?

Without warning, tears flooded Matthew's eyes. First he'd lost his father at Blackwater Lake, then again in Izzy Webster's living room. He'd never felt so bereft.

Memories of his dad, the solid man who raised him, washed over him. The wooden animals, carved with such love. His reassurances after his son's attempt as a teenager to clear the hoard. Whatever kind of man he'd been when he murdered Kerensa, as a husband and father Joe Stanyer hadn't shown signs of a violent temper. His decision to ditch the booze, his marriage to Evie, becoming a parent – all those factors must have accounted for the change. But nothing could alter the fact he'd once killed a pregnant woman.

Suck it up, he told himself. What choice did he have, other than to accept the truth?

Time to return downstairs. He washed his hands, struck by his face in the bathroom mirror. Grief stared back at him, evident in the pallor of his skin, the pinched set of his mouth, forcing him to avert his eyes and head for the door.

As he passed his aunt's bedroom, idle curiosity made him glance inside. Moonlight illuminated the furniture, glinting off a framed photo on the dressing table. Matthew's feet halted in mid-stride, his attention arrested by what he saw. He padded softly across the carpet, picking up the photo, its silver surround cool under his fingers. Kerensa Price laughed up at the camera. At her side, Izzy was also smiling, but her gaze wasn't aimed at whoever was taking the photo. Instead, she was staring at the other woman, her expression one of adoration.

Shit. Izzy Webster had been in love with Kerensa Price.

As though his hand was moving through treacle, Matthew replaced the photo. Behind it sat a large wooden box, its lid ornately carved with flowers, a rope of beads emerging from its depths. A jewellery box, then. He opened it to expose a tangle of bangles, necklaces and hair clasps. As his fingers rifled through the box's contents, his brain certain of what he'd find, a flash of blue caught his eye. A string of sapphires set in a gold chain. Kerensa's missing bracelet.

Chapter 13 - *Bloodied*

When Matthew returned downstairs, his aunt was still in the kitchen. On hearing his feet on the stairs, she shouted, 'I've put a chocolate cake on the table. Help yourself.'

His throat tight, he sat on the sofa. Wedged between his thigh and the armrest was the photo from her bedroom, its frame digging into his flesh. Izzy Webster breezed in, setting two mugs of coffee on the side table. She cut herself a slice of cake before joining him on the sofa, gesturing towards the remaining plate. 'You're not hungry?'

Matthew looked straight at his aunt. 'You loved Kerensa Price.'

She paled. 'What are you saying? Of course not.'

'Don't deny it.' He held the photo towards her. 'I can see it in your face. You were in love with her.'

'You went into my bedroom? How dare you—'

'I found her bracelet as well.'

He watched as she swallowed, saw the tears creep into her eyes. No anger remained in her voice when she spoke, only pain. 'You don't understand.'

He did, though, only too well. 'My father didn't kill Kerensa, did he?'

'No.' A stifled sob.

'You exaggerated about his temper.'

She nodded, a barely perceptible tilt of her head.

'It was you, wasn't it? You killed her.'

Izzy's expression betrayed decades of guilt, before she finally burst into tears. After that, only her anguish sounded in the room.

At last she sobbed herself dry. Her body still, Izzy stared at Matthew. 'Now you know.'

'What happened? Tell me. No lies this time.'

His aunt straightened her back, squared her shoulders. Silence for a few seconds. Then: 'I was fourteen when I realised I was a lesbian. I never told anyone, though. Hard enough to admit it to myself.'

'Because of your parents?'

'Yes. Mum and Dad – they were rigid about such things. Homosexuality was a sin, unnatural, against God's holy plan. Faggots and dykes were destined to burn in hell for all eternity.'

'Did you tell Evie?'

'No. She was two years younger, remember, and I didn't think a twelve-year-old would understand. Besides, I fought it. Told myself I couldn't be gay; how, if I prayed hard enough, God would relieve me of my sin. But He didn't. At seventeen I met David, and he seemed the answer to my prayers. Good-looking, kind, and so in love with me. I married him at eighteen and spent the next two years regretting it.'

'So you divorced him.'

'Yes. Our marriage never stood a chance; I tried so hard, but I couldn't bear him to touch me.

By the time we split up, my parents were dead and Evie was dating your father. And she'd rekindled her friendship with Kerensa.'

'That was how the two of you met?'

'Yes. Evie said she bumped into her at Blackwater Park one day. Kerensa had told her she was unhappy at home, that she'd never got over her parents' divorce. Sometimes she came to the park she'd loved as a child to escape her mother's nagging. Evie invited me over one time. Said Kerensa would be joining us. How we'd drink beer and party at Blackwater Lake.' A smile lit his aunt's face. 'I'll never forget seeing her that evening. That white skin, her red hair—' Izzy swallowed. 'I fell for her, hook, line and sinker.'

'And Kerensa? Did she fall for you too?'

'Yes. At first, anyway. She stared at me that night and didn't stop. Evie and Joe didn't notice, what with being so wrapped up in each other. Which left Kerensa and me free to talk. Somewhere along the way I fell in love.'

Matthew understood. An abusive childhood, a failed marriage, few friends – Izzy must have been hellishly lonely. Vulnerable. Ripe for becoming besotted with Kerensa Price.

'We met again the next night. She swooped on me as soon as she walked through the door. I wasn't her first, of course. Not even her tenth. She'd started sleeping around, with girls as well as boys, after her mum and dad split up. The way we made love, though – I convinced myself her wild days were behind her. Stupid of me.' Bitterness tinged Izzy's voice.

'She wasn't as committed as you?'

'Not by a long shot. We saw each other a few times after that. I got clingy, needy. She told me I was suffocating her. I persuaded myself that if she understood how much I loved her, everything would be fine.' Pain choked her words.

'The night she died, Joe and Evie picked her up from where she lived, like they always did. We were at Blackwater Park, by the lake, the closed-off part where nobody else ever came. Joe normally supplied the beer or lager, but that evening he brought Pepsi instead, along with food. Evie wanted some pickle, so the two of them went to buy a jar of Branston's. When we were alone I told Kerensa I wanted to be with her forever. She laughed at me. Said I should get a life.' Her fingers twisted in her lap.

'So you killed her?'

'Not then. I convinced myself she hadn't meant to hurt me, that she was confused about loving another woman. I said as much. That's when she told me I'd been a fling, that it was over. How she was five months gone – not that she looked it – by one of several possible guys. She hadn't told her mother, though.'

'She'd decided to keep the baby?'

'Yes. Said she wanted the love a child would give her.' Izzy's mouth twisted. 'Why couldn't she get that from me?'

'That must have hurt.'

'It did. I felt so stupid. She betrayed me, then mocked me with it.' A hard note edged into

Izzy Webster's voice. 'She told me I was a loser. Well, I lost it all right.'

'What happened?'

'Joe had brought a kitchen knife for the food. I grabbed it and stabbed her in the belly. Such shock on her face as the blade slid in.' Her lips twisted again. 'I held one hand over her mouth to stop her screaming. She was smaller, not as strong, unable to fight back. I kept stabbing her, in her chest, stomach, everywhere. The only thought in my head was how much I hated her. When I finally stopped, she was dead.'

Christ. The scene, in all its bloody horror, played vividly in his head. 'And when my parents got back? They found you like that?'

'Yes. Evie became hysterical when she saw me drenched in blood. She had no idea about Kerensa and me; I'd not long been able to admit being gay to myself, remember. I'll never forget her face as I screamed how the bitch had cheated on me. I told her Kerensa deserved everything she got. The little whore should have kept her legs shut.'

His mother's words. Far from admitting her own guilt, she'd been parroting that of her sister.

'Evie was afraid the police would think Joe killed her, what with the knife crime charge. She told me he'd asked her to marry him after she discovered she was pregnant. The reason they were drinking Pepsi, not Pilsner. I offered to come clean, confess to killing her, but Evie couldn't bear to think of me being jailed for life.'

'She agreed to cover up what you did?'

'Yes. Because she loved me, always had. She remembered how I did my best to protect her against our parents.' Izzy wiped away a tear. 'My anger had evaporated by then; all I could remember was how beautiful Kerensa had been, how much I adored her. It was wrong, I realise that. I did something terrible, and I should have paid the price. But I was twenty-two, with no experience of the world, and I knew I'd not survive in prison. The thought terrified me.'

'My father disposed of the body?'

'Yes. He ran to his car to get rope from the boot. Whilst he was gone, I took Kerensa's bracelet from her wrist. I craved a part of her to keep forever, you see.' She sniffed back more tears. 'When Joe returned, he wrapped her in the tarpaulin, securing it with the rope. We searched for rocks to weigh her down, but didn't find any. Joe discovered what to do once he'd lowered Kerensa into the lake, found out the bottom dipped at that point. Then he spotted the tree roots leading into the water, so he fastened the tarpaulin to one of them. Said it would keep her from floating away.'

'He was right.'

'Yes. Well, up until now. I suppose the rope must have rotted after so long in the water.'

Matthew stayed silent. No point in revealing the part he'd played in freeing the corpse.

'We were lucky. A heavy thunderstorm started not long afterwards. Plenty of blood had splashed on the ground as well as the tarpaulin, but I guess it all got washed away. Not that anyone looked for Kerensa at Blackwater Park.'

'You never considered moving her body? Burying her somewhere else?'

'Too risky. The lake was as good a place as any to hide her.'

'What about her handbag?'

'She'd left it beside a tree. We didn't spot it until she was in the water.'

'Mum took it?'

'Said she'd dispose of it later. Seems that didn't happen.'

'No,' Matthew said. 'She kept it instead. I'm guessing it spawned her hoarding obsession.'

Tears slid down Izzy's cheeks. 'Something broke that night between Evie and me.'

'What do you mean?'

'Oh, she still loved me. But she said she didn't recognise the blood-drenched woman in front of her. How she'd never forget the horror of what I'd done. She'd help me, make sure I didn't go to prison, but said I couldn't play a part in her life any longer. Not now she was pregnant, starting a new life, quitting the booze. I was devastated but she wouldn't budge.'

'You didn't see your sister again?'

'No. Evie stuck to her word. Not that I didn't try. I went to the house, like I told you, a month later. Phoned as well, but they'd changed the number. I sent those cards, but she never responded.'

'Mum didn't suffer from jealousy issues, did she? You made that up.'

'Yes. Evie knew Joe loved her, would never cheat on her.'

'It was you who broke into my parents' house, wasn't it? As well as peep through the window. Why?'

Izzy blew out a breath. 'I thought there might be some evidence I could destroy. I hadn't bargained on all the junk, though.'

A question nagged at the back of Matthew's mind. 'Why did you stop sending the cards?'

'Everything got too much. The guilt over Kerensa, missing Evie – it built inside me like a pressure cooker. Four year later I suffered a mental breakdown. Spent a long time on a psychiatric ward. When I recovered, I stopped trying to contact my sister, for my sanity's sake.' She grimaced. 'I'm worthless, a sinner, like my parents always said.'

Matthew took a deep breath. 'You realise I'll have to inform the police?'

Her expression soured even further. 'I was afraid you'd say that.'

Too late, he clocked the cake knife in her hand, the raw fury spiking in her eyes. His left side registered pain, sharp and piercing, the shock rendering him immobile for a second. Giving Izzy the chance to stab him again, this time on the right. The pain was excruciating, hot daggers of torment burning through his torso. His aunt's breathing was harsh, her eyes wide and mad. Her demented face offered him a glimpse of what Kerensa Price must have seen before she died.

Matthew collapsed to the floor, clutching his stomach, his eyes darting around for possible weapons. Then he spotted the heavy glass lamp on the sideboard. Yes. That's how he'd bring down this bitch. His feet kicked out, landing a vicious blow to Izzy's ankle, knocking her legs from under her, giving him his chance. With one hand he dragged the lamp from the sideboard, seizing it as it fell to the floor. Before his aunt could get up, he cracked it down as hard as he could on the side of her head. The blow wasn't enough to knock her unconscious, but it bought him the time he needed. Crawling through the doorway, Matthew staggered to his feet once he reached the hall, twisting open the front door and lurching onto the path leading to the gate.

Noises came from the house behind him; muttered curses, along with the sounds of his aunt hauling herself up. His stomach throbbed, a dull ache replacing the sharp pain of before. On his shirt, two wet circles bloomed crimson. With shaking and bloodied fingers, Matthew pulled out his mobile. Time for an ambulance. The police, too.

He never got that far. Instead, his legs crumpled under him and his vision turned black.

Chapter 14 - *Ashes*

The moment Matthew arrived home from hospital, accompanied by Lauren, he took her straight to bed. Sex was out of the question, given his wounds, but it didn't matter; right now, he needed the comfort she offered. His girlfriend had been a rock, despite her shock at receiving a call saying he'd been stabbed, was recovering in hospital. A lazy Sunday afternoon drifted by; they lay together, legs entwined, arms around each other. Everything melted from his mind: Kerensa's bracelet, the savagery of her murder, the cake knife piercing his flesh. All that remained was Lauren. They dozed for a while.

Now awake, she folded her arms behind her head, eyeballing Matthew. 'Your stitches OK, babe?'

'Fine.' His body was sore, he'd lost a fair bit of blood, but the cake knife had missed his vital organs.

'Sheesh, Matt. You're lucky to be alive.' She kissed him hard. 'Thank God that passer-by saw you, called an ambulance.'

'Amen to that.'

'I've been wondering. Did Izzy Webster's illness have anything to do with her attacking you?'

'Might have done. Certain brain tumours can cause aggressive behaviour, or so they told me at the hospital. And I'd cornered her, don't forget.'

'Have you sorted everything with the police?'

'Yes. Gave them the cuttings, Kerensa's handbag and the photos of Izzy with her.' He'd lied, telling both Connelly and Lauren those things were the reason he'd confronted his aunt, how they'd been in the very last box he checked. 'He's also got her signed confession, along with the sapphire bracelet.'

'She told him the same story she did you?'

'Yes. Didn't doubt she would. The man's scarier than a rabid Rottweiler.'

'Will there be a trial?'

'No need. She'll appear in court, sure, but plead guilty.'

'Probably relieved it's out in the open,' Lauren said. 'She won't serve much time, right?'

'Not with the brain tumour. She only has a few months to live.'

'Doesn't seem fair. For her to evade a life sentence, I mean.'

'I don't think she has.'

'What do you mean?'

Matthew drew in a deep breath. 'For thirty-five years she's locked herself in a prison of her own making. No relationship, no children. Estranged from her sister, never knowing her nephew. A mental breakdown. She punished herself far more severely than the law ever could.'

*****

That evening, Matthew polished off Lauren's latest pie creation she'd brought from her flat. Chicken and leek with a hint of garlic. He pushed back his plate. 'Think that's my favourite so far.'

'You're hired as my taste tester. Play your cards right and it might be a permanent position.' Her voice stilled as she stared at the TV screen. The evening news had started, the reporter the same one as before.

'Following the confession of a Bristol woman to the murder of Kerensa Price, the victim's mother says she can now die in peace. Hannah Price is receiving hospice care for a terminal illness. She is too ill to talk to the media, but her brother will read a statement from the family.' The camera cut to the man Matthew had seen before.

'My sister wishes to express her satisfaction that her daughter's murderer is in custody.' Peter Moore's voice was steady, despite the emotion in his face. 'For thirty-five years she has suffered a living hell. All she wanted was the chance to give her child a decent funeral, something that is now possible. Although she is gravely ill, she is determined to attend the cremation.'

'Mr. Moore, has your sister said anything about Isabelle Webster, the woman who confessed to killing Kerensa?'

Peter Moore raised his eyes from Hannah's statement, his expression hard. 'She is relieved this woman has admitted her guilt. However, she cannot find it in her heart to forgive her. Neither can I.' His mouth compressed into a grim line. 'Isabelle Webster deprived my niece of her life. Nothing can compensate for that.'

Beside him, Lauren snorted. 'Why should anyone forgive her? The not knowing – it must have been agony for Hannah Price.'

'Not sure it's that simple, babe.'

'What do you mean?'

He pulled her close. 'I never told you what Evie and Izzy endured as kids. Horrific stuff. Beatings, abuse. Mum had an outlet; she rebelled, did the wild child thing. Izzy, though – she suppressed her emotions instead.'

'Until they eventually exploded. Christ, Matt, her childhood must have really screwed her up.' Lauren shook her head. 'I'm surprised your mother escaped with just a hoarding obsession.'

'Her hoarding wasn't an escape, babe. Think about it. The narrowness of her life, chained to that house. Imprisoned by all the junk.'

For decades, Matthew thought, his mother concealed Izzy's secret, but in doing so, she paid a terrible price. Forced apart from her sister, the trauma of Kerensa's murder the trigger, Evie embarked on her hoarding obsession. She'd started with the photos, the cuttings, the handbag and purse. Buried them deep, suffocating them with junk, ensuring they never saw daylight. From such roots, the hoard had grown. Stealthy as bindweed, over the decades it choked the house and its occupants. Was he now free of its stranglehold, Matthew wondered?

'As though she wore her home as a security blanket,' Lauren said. 'By cramming it with stuff, she was pulling it around her. To keep the world at bay.'

'I reckon you're right.'

'Perhaps your father wanted the truth to come out one day. Could be why he didn't dispose of the evidence from the hoard.'

Matthew hadn't considered that. 'It's a strong possibility.'

'They stayed in Blackwater because of his job, didn't they?' A crease appeared in his girlfriend's brow as the thought struck her. 'He needed to guard Kerensa's body.'

'Explains why he ended his life there, along with my mother's. The events at Blackwater Lake defined their whole existence, not to mention Izzy's.'

'You're not kidding. Christ, your grandparents messed up so many lives. Those of their daughters, your father, Hannah Price. Not to mention Kerensa's.'

'Mine too.' Matthew drew in a deep breath. 'The hoard – you say it was a security blanket for my mother. For me, though, it was a plastic bag over the head, suffocating me. You know what, though? Now I'm grateful to it.'

She pulled back to stare at him. 'How so?'

He chose his words with care. 'Over the years, the hoard assumed monstrous proportions in my head. I blamed it for not having friends as a kid, my strained relationship with Mum and Dad, you name it. But clearing their stuff brought me closer to them.'

'Because of what you found?'

'Yes. Weird how selective our memories can be. I'd focused on everything wrong with my childhood, forgetting the good stuff. Like the wooden animals Dad carved for me. How Mum kept every Christmas and birthday card I ever sent them. They may not have had much money, but I had food to eat, clothes to wear, a warm bed. Parents who loved each other, who never abused me.'

'Lots to be grateful for there.'

'Yes. Every box I threw away, every cupboard I emptied – it was as though I was peeling layers of resentment off myself. I'd hated the hoard for so long, and now it was disappearing. Guess I cleared the crap in my head as well.'

*****

The following week, Matthew stood in his parents' garden. Behind him, his mother's roses shivered in the breeze, their petals a soft pink. The weak July sunshine struggled to break through the clouds, the summer being what his father would have described as nippy. Beside him, Lauren held a black glass jar, the size and shape of those stocked in old-fashioned sweet shops. An identical one stood beside his feet, along with a trowel. Yesterday he'd collected his parents' remains from Canford Crematorium, the place where, at eleven o'clock, Hannah Price would bid goodbye to her daughter. At the same time,

Matthew planned to bury Joe and Evie Stanyer's ashes amongst the roses they loved. The symmetry of it pleased him.

'This is a beautiful idea,' Lauren said. 'You're doing the right thing, babe.'

'I thought of scattering them at Blackwater Park. But Blackwater is where Kerensa died. Hardly surprising that Mum refused to go anywhere near the place. My parents spent decades in this house. They were happy here.'

Silence for a while. The wind whipped a few petals from the roses, wafting their scent towards him.

Lauren glanced at her watch. 'It's time.'

Matthew unscrewed the lid from his father's remains before stepping over to the rose beds. His hands steady, he tilted the jar. A stream of ashes poured onto the earth, some blown back against his jeans by the breeze. With the trowel, he dug his father deep into the Blackwater soil he'd loved. Then he did the same with his mother.

He stood beside Lauren, his arm around her, absorbing the moment.

After a minute, he pulled her closer. 'Remember what we discussed? About Crete?'

Lauren's expression grew serious. 'I'm willing to give it a go. If you are.'

'I'm game. Time to put Bristol behind me.' He'd not regret it, of that he was certain. His mother's hoard belonged to the past, as did the dark waters that drowned his father. From his future, the blue seas of Greece beckoned.

At his feet, a few flakes of ash fluttered. Then the breeze carried them high above the fence, blowing them into the distance.

POSTSCRIPT

I hope you enjoyed *Blackwater Lake*! If so, please consider leaving a review on Amazon or Goodreads.

For more information about me and my books, you can visit my website at www.maggiejamesfiction.com, or follow me on Facebook, Twitter, Amazon, BookBub, LinkedIn or Pinterest.

My newsletter is sent out monthly to members of my Special Readers' group. All subscribers receive a free ebook copy of *Blackwater Lake*. I offer discounts on my novels and those of other authors, book recommendations and snippets from my personal life. I respect your privacy and will never share your e-mail address with any third parties. Why not sign up today at my website www.maggiejamesfiction.com? Thank you!

ABOUT THE AUTHOR

Maggie James is a British author who lives near Newcastle-upon-Tyne. She writes psychological suspense novels.

Before turning her hand to writing, Maggie worked mainly as an accountant, with a diversion into practising as a nutritional therapist. Diet and health remain high on her list of interests, along with travel. Accountancy does not, but then it never did. The urge to pack a bag and go off travelling is always lurking in the background! When not writing, going to the gym, practising yoga or travelling, Maggie can be found seeking new four-legged friends to pet; animals are a lifelong love!

Join Maggie's mailing list to receive the latest news and discounts. To sign up, visit:
www.maggiejamesfiction.com.

Facebook: Maggie James Fiction
Twitter: @mjamesfiction

Printed in Great Britain
by Amazon

79149457R00075